G R JORDAN

The Darkness At Dillingham

An Austerley & Kirkgordon Adventure #2

To Chrisella,
a passion for language I'd never seen before.

Contents

Prologue

What the hell are they doing to her, thought Wilson. In all his experience, never had he seen such a transformation, such an impact on a person's visage and such a draining of colour from someone's cheeks. Many times he had read about weird and unusual things in his line of work but to see magic at first hand was totally different.

And magic it was, but not of the illusionist's variety. No, this was old and deep, taught by dark forces in the bleakest of nights to desperate souls who had abandoned all science and all goodly gods. Clearing the island of those frog creatures had been nothing compared to this.

He glanced at his watch, making a mental note: 2 am. His boss liked detail so he knew this report was going to take a while. He'd be lucky to be in his bed by eight. Maybe nine. For six weeks he had been watching the place for the department but only this week had there been a slip-up. His cover story – a cleaner in the care home – had allowed him access to all the residents' rooms and he had seen the little brooch by their beds.

The brooch was unremarkable, made from emerald but poor in quality. The fastenings had rusted and the clasp operated poorly. Framed by some false diamonds, the emerald had a small plaque above it with one word: "*Huthnamac*". The common man would not have thought much about what meaning there was but Wilson was a graduate in older languages and had been trained to spot the out-of-place.

The first room he had seen the brooch in was Mr Melville's. An austere gentleman from Derbyshire, slightly eccentric, he was in the home for his own comfort and protection. Life stressed him, and he constantly complained about the boys ruining the flowers. Of course, there were no boys and the flowers were flourishing quite well for the time of year. Despite his happy madness, Mr Melville was physically very well. At least he had been. The day after Wilson had seen the brooch, Mr Melville was dead.

Wilson had broken into the hospital to examine the body before the autopsy. Mr Melville was white but with a faded look, like cheap emulsion. The life had been drained from him. And yet, two days later, the autopsy report said he had died from natural causes. The coroner must be in on it, thought Wilson.

During his next cleaning round he had noticed the brooch again, in the room of Mrs Moor – vibrant, but once again quite mad. Wilson had notified his superior and prepared to stake out her room.

They had come for her at midnight when the home was in shut-down – doors locked and residents asleep. Watching closely, he saw them place her into a car. Mrs Moor was asleep, or more likely drugged, for she gave no resistance. He followed them up to the hill at the edge of town. There had been several people guarding the site, unseen to the untrained eye but for those in Wilson's line of work they were quite obvious.

Mrs Moor had been taken up to the highest outlook of the

bay, a place called "Gibbet Point". Six people stood around her. She was sitting in a wheelchair. They laid hands upon her and chanted a language that even Wilson didn't recognize.

The wind picked up and a chill blew right through him. Several crows took to the air and rabbits left their burrows, fleeing down the hill. As the chanting grew, Wilson watched Mrs Moor age drastically. Her skin lost its rosy glow and turned pale. Her hair greyed before his eyes. Lines spread out across her face and her neck tightened. With a start, her eyes flicked open and shrunk back into their sockets. Can I stop this, thought Wilson, removing his gun from its holster. Any firing will bring the lookouts. The boss wouldn't be happy if Mrs Moor was saved but the protagonists managed to flee. The greater good, he always said. His boss was the finest he'd known in their line of work, but he was also a cold, hard bastard when he needed to be. A consummate professional, they called him. Sorry dear, thought Wilson, you're going to be sacrificed for the greater good.

Something, some... substance, left Mrs Moor's body. Wilson didn't understand what he was seeing. It displaced the light around her, as if her outline had dropped out of focus. The substance continued upwards and coagulated above her head before racing towards a large metal cage at the lookout point. Then... nothing. Wilson looked back at Mrs Moor. She was drained of all colour. It was as if she had aged another twenty years.

Time to go, thought Wilson. He turned quietly, scanning for the poorly hidden guards. But there was a figure just five feet away. At least, he thought it was a figure. There was that same displacement of the light, like looking through watery eyes. This time, it had a shape. It was human and nearly seven feet tall. Was it wearing a tri-cornered hat? Wilson saw an arm pull something from its side. Then there was a slash with a blurred sword. Wilson threw his hands up to block the attack but felt the invisible blade cut into him.

With the dark setting in, Wilson's last sight was a blurred, colourless face, almost transparent, but with eyes that burned with hunger and passion. And hatred. With his last act, Wilson reached inside his pocket, pressed a secret button, and murmured "Havers".

Mind the Gap

Kirkgordon pulled his bow case from the top rack of the carriage and sat down briefly, waiting for the train to stop at the platform. Tired from an early start, he had taken three trains to arrive at Dillingham-on-sea, some six hundred miles from his starting point on the east coast of Scotland. What had possessed Havers to send Austerley all the way down here? At the last minute, too. Surely there were equally good care homes in Scotland in which to prepare someone for a prosthetic foot? Especially as the work to fit the new appendage would take place in Glasgow. Madness!

With his bow case and small rucksack slung over either shoulder, Kirkgordon stepped off the train and took in the platform sheltered under a Victorian roof of corrugated form. There were few travellers about, no doubt something that would be remedied in the commuter rush of the evening. A small coffee cart stood at one side with a lacklustre teenager lounging behind it, fizzy pop in hand. Oh well, I'll guess I'll wait 'til the town for a decent cup, thought Kirkgordon.

Once clear of the station, Kirkgordon walked up a tree-lined road and stood at the summit of a small hill, looking down on the town by the bay that was to be his home for the next two weeks. At the shoreline there was a wide beach with the occasional walker enjoying the sunshine. There was a bottleneck of slow-moving cars leading into the town and a tight inner section of buildings with extremely narrow streets. Rising from the centre of this inner section was a church spire, and Kirkgordon resolved to see what time the services were on. Since the events on the island he had started seeking out a place to worship, a rekindling of his dormant faith.

The island. He shuddered at the recollection of the demon from the deep, not to mention the dragon who had ripped off Austerley's foot. A pissed-off, three-headed dragon that was still on the loose. And trying to kill Austerley.

For the last two weeks, Kirkgordon had been staying with his estranged wife, Alana, trying to mend relationships with his family. In fairness, there had been a lot of love, even sexual love, but also a lot of resentment, nightmares and rage. Alana had tried to be compassionate but, in reality, he wasn't ready to live with anyone full-time yet. And neither was Austerley. So for two weeks at a time, Kirkgordon had a babysitting job. Babysitting Austerley. Two weeks on, two weeks off. At least I don't have to share with him this week, thought Kirkgordon. Normally, the odd couple shared a flat at the expense of their employer, SETAA, the Supernatural and Elder Threat Assessment Agency, a hushed-up government body.

On the walk into town, Kirkgordon spotted a small café and sat down inside to escape the noise of overheating cars. This wasn't like Scotland – too many damn people living here. Ordering a latte, he picked up a local map to peruse. After quickly locating the bird sanctuary and the small natural spring the town was famous for, he studied the map closely for more useful locations. The library, supermarket, leisure centre and pubs were marked and also a viewing spot called "Gibbet Point". It seemed to be a reasonable walk so he thought he might take a stroll before Austerley arrived on the late evening train, but as it was already mid-afternoon, Kirkgordon reckoned he should find his digs first.

The Shady Palm Guest House lacked the trees of its name and also lacked an en-suite bathroom. The elderly female proprietor was friendly enough and gave the promise of a large fry-up every morning, but the room had such a soft bed that Kirkgordon thought he might sink into its depths never to return. The drab pink bedspread didn't do much for it either.

Forsaking his room, Kirkgordon set out on the stroll he had planned and a fresh breeze hit his face as he approached the shoreline. The salt air appealed to him at first but then brought back more memories of the island. He found himself checking the sea for tentacles. Focus, dammit, focus.

The rising climb to the viewpoint helped energize him. At the top of the climb was an odd-looking cage, swinging gently in the breeze, and the remains of a small building, now reduced to an archway. As he stood looking out to sea he began to feel optimistic that he could use these two weeks to recover. After all, how difficult would it be to babysit Austerley? There was nothing here to fuel Austerley's obsession with the occult. Time to recuperate and repair some damage.

Something caught his eye on his way back down. Beyond the path, the grass was closely cut for about a foot before turning wild. His attention had been grabbed by a flash of red against the green, and he strode over to examine it. It was blood, dried blood, and in a significant quantity. Kirkgordon wondered what had happened here. Probably some toddler fell and bashed his head, his self-preservation reassured him, but his heart disagreed. Something kicked in him.

Not much I can do about anything anyway, he thought. I have no idea what happened so best just leave it. But his years of running security and protection details had given Kirkgordon a nose for the out-of-place, and it was hard to drown out what his experience was telling him. Still, that coffee had been good, time for another. He made his way back to the town.

He was recognized by the barista at the coffee house and engaged in a pleasant chat before retracing his previous steps back to the train station. Although SETAA would gladly foot the bill for a taxi, Kirkgordon was enjoying the freedom to roam. The air was fresh with a distinct, crispy saltiness to it and, breathing deeply, he felt invigorated. Then his impending meeting crossed his mind.

When Kirkgordon had last left Austerley, the air between them had been thick with anger. Feeling guilty, Kirkgordon had even asked to be forgiven for trying to kill Austerley during the demonic ritual on the island, but the former asylum detainee wasn't to be moved. He just won't listen to reason, thought Kirkgordon, nothing is ever his fault. Serves the stupid arse right for getting me involved in this occult nonsense in the first place.

Standing on the platform, Kirkgordon read the overhead display and saw that the train was delayed. Typical. He searched for the coffee cart from earlier and noticed it had moved to the other platform, so he descended the steps and followed the underground tunnel, ignoring the smell of urine in the subway. Emerging on the other side, he announced cheerily to the teenage server that he required a latte.

"Got black only, machine's off. Or I can give you this UHT stuff." Kirkgordon smiled wearily. Black it would have to be.

Austerley had rarely left his bed while Kirkgordon had been babysitting him, instead plaguing Kirkgordon with his constant demands. The mad expert of the occult had also been requesting various books from dubious libraries around the world, all vetted by Havers, SETAA's top man, of course. The incident on the island hadn't dampened Austerley's taste for the strange, but it had reduced his mobility. Havers had suggested a prosthetic and Austerley had readily agreed. With a date two weeks away for the fitting of the limb, this sudden relocation seemed weird to Kirkgordon but hey-ho. Two weeks of sun and Mr Grumpy courtesy of the taxpayer shouldn't be sniffed at. Better this than being stuck in the flat with him.

Austerley was so damn gung-ho with these dark matters they looked into that Kirkgordon had nicknamed him Indy, although it was a bit ridiculous. Austerley was too heavy and slow to be like Harrison Ford – more like a model T Ford with his deep jowls and rotund belly. And to think he calls me Churchy, thought Kirkgordon. Just because I believe there's a big man looking out for me. One thing's for sure in all this nonsense Indy's got me into: I'm looking for the light again. Definitely looking. I must check out the service on Sunday.

A degree in sound analysis was needed to understand the tannoy announcement but, on looking at the electronic boards, Kirkgordon deduced that Austerley's train was approaching. The smell of diesel heralded its arrival and the train of four carriages pulled into the station proper. The carriages were obviously old stock and none opened automatically. Kirkgordon recognized a head appearing at one of the windows. Having pushed the window down, the man inside sought a fixture for opening the door. On finding it, he seemed to struggle for an age.

For three minutes, Kirkgordon watched the man struggle and laughed at his efforts. The man's face grew redder and sweat started to form on his forehead; his hair became matted and its weak curls dampened so it looked like he was wearing a poorly made wig. This was fun.

The train whistled and Kirkgordon tried to wave down a platform attendant but there was none. There was a judder and the train started to move. Ah, bollocks, thought Kirkgordon, I am not chasing him in a taxi. He leapt onto the little wooden step at the bottom of the door as the carriage went past. He placed one hand inside the door and the other on the collar at the back of the man's neck. Kirkgordon pulled hard and yanked him head first out of the carriage, spinning him clear and onto his back. He then dived into the carriage and threw the luggage out of the window. Just as the carriage was clearing the end of the platform and picking up reasonable speed, Kirkgordon leapt out head first, landing in a forward roll.

Standing, he looked back at the carnage he had caused. Four pieces of luggage were scattered down the platform, one of them open, exposing large white Y-fronts. Beyond these cases was a man in a bomber jacket and a purple knitted hat which reminded Kirkgordon of a tea cosy. His legs were inside jogging bottoms and one foot had a cheap-looking white trainer on it. The other leg ended in a stump. Dammit, I'd better help him up, thought Kirkgordon.

"I don't need your bloody help. What the hell was that anyway? Can't you just help people normally?"

"Good to see you too, Indy," answered Kirkgordon. "I thought you might have had a spell or a rune to open the door with."

"You can sod off. It's not that flippin' easy when you only

have one foot. I was just going to press the alarm when you ejected me. Anyway, where are my sticks?"

"Sticks?"

"Yeah, bloody sticks. I don't just hop about. Remember, I use my crutches to walk with."

"Ah. Didn't see them."

"They were beside the door, dammit. And who's luggage is all that?"

"Yours."

"Mine? No, just the small case further up. The rest ain't mine, Churchy."

"Get off it, those are your Y-fronts, Indy."

"As if. Look at the stuff in there with them. I don't wear bras, do I?"

"Arse! Well, maybe you should. Anyway, get up."

"I do need a hand with that, as because of some clown I've no sticks." Kirkgordon reached down and put Austerley's arm around his neck. He then took the excess luggage to the stationmaster with some cock and bull story about a teenager. Ordering a taxi, he thought how peaceful the day had been before Austerley's arrival. Here we go, he thought.

Care Home for an Austerley

W ell, this looks like a right dump. If I'd known Havers would make us go NHS, I would have paid for private," said Austerley on exiting the taxi. He was leaning on the taxi roof with both hands steadying himself and feeling lopsided without his sticks. Removing Austerley's bag with one hand, Kirkgordon manoeuvred himself under Austerley's shoulder. Like failed three-legged race competitors they fell twice on the way to reception.

"Ah, it must be Mr Austerley. Apologies for not meeting you at the door but your secretary failed to inform us of your arrival time. If your manservant would be so kind as to take your bag to room twelve? That's down the corridor and take a left, fifty metres and on the left."

Austerley balanced in total disbelief. The man in front of him wore a purple cravat over a bright yellow shirt with a pair of mid-blue corduroy trousers setting off his purple cowboy boots. Kirkgordon, affronted by the manservant jibe, now chortled to himself as he carried the luggage away. Austerley tried to retreat as the man advanced towards him with a hand extended but found he was unable to escape without hopping away.

"We don't get many gentlemen in as fine fettle as yourself, except for the odd soldier resting up after injuries. Always a boon that. But with your rugged complexion I'm sure you'll be ready for the prosthetic in no time at all. Now let me get you a wheelchair. Can't have you hopping to and fro all day, can we? I'd have thought they would have provided some sticks for you but then that's the NHS nowadays. My dear Pappy would turn in his grave if he could see the state it's got into today. Just a nightmare from what it was. Bring back the matrons, I say."

Austerley didn't say anything. He knew he didn't want to but was also keenly aware that even if he did, there were no spaces available in which to insert any words. His mind was still reeling from the primary colour shock of the man's outfit. Pondering how his nightmares at this point seemed so much tamer than real life, Austerley was suddenly swept off his feet. Pushing the wheelchair against the back of Austerley's knees, the manager had effectively skittled him into the chair. Before he could recover, the man was leaning over him and continuing with his introduction.

"Now, my name's Mr Hammond, Graham Hammond Esquire, but you can call me Grahamsey. We all have our little family names here and you'll be no exception. So it's Grahamsey. And what do I call you?"

The sudden pause in the conversation took Austerley un-aware and he took a moment to realize he was meant to speak. When the question had connected to his brain, he decided this man was getting nothing from him. No, not someone like this. I mean, I don't mind a feminine side to a man, but what was this, he thought.

"Cat got your tongue? Or maybe you're just a shy one during the introductions. Hey, that's alright, we can all be like that sometimes. Well, except me, obviously. I'm what you might call your extrovert. Little Grahamsey here, doing the do and all that, just for you. Oh, I do make myself laugh some times. Tell you what, I'll just call you Aussie."

I'm getting pummelled by a fashion car crash, thought Austerley. Not that I'm God's gift to fashion, but come on. He looks like a children's TV character.

"Indy, just call him Indy." Kirkgordon had returned.

"Oh, Indy is it? Now that's something. From what dark deeds of the past does this rugged man get this title then? Please tell. I'm all ears."

"It's his Harrison Ford looks that do it. Have you ever seen such a chiselled chin?" Graham seemed somewhat unconvinced but rallied superbly to extend a hand to Kirkgordon and shake it. I daren't tell him it's Austerley's cavalier attitude to the dark forces of this world and beyond that get him his nickname. Austerley's probably strange enough for this guy without adding anything extra.

"Well, I'm Graham Hammond, or Grahamsey, as I was telling..." – Graham paused briefly as if checking he wasn't just missing the joke – "telling Indy. We all stick to our little family names, as I call them. So, we have Indy and Grahamsey, and you are...?"

"Kirkgordon."

"Well, nice to meet you, Kirk. I used to know an excellent snooker player in Blackpool called Kirk. He could knock any ball into a pocket with his walnut cue, and they don't make them for fun. He was quite a hustler too and a wild night out, used to have us all in stitches. Got hit by a bus on the promenade after winning a donkey derby as the rear end. Tragic."

Austerley's face was frozen. Crystallized in disbelief, he choked at the donkey derby reference to such a degree that Graham produced a handkerchief.

"Actually, it's Kirkgordon. As in a surname."

"Right. Well, Mr Kirkgordon, what shall we call you?"

"Churchy," Austerley butted in.

"Oh, a minister," observed Graham.

"No, no," insisted Kirkgordon, "but Churchy's fine if you want to use it. Indy and I just have a different view of the end times, that's all."

"Well, the only end time I worry about is closing time at the pub. Mind you, they're not too sharp round these parts, you can usually get a few stacked up if you're so inclined. Maybe I'll take Indy here out for a few glasses of champers tonight." Kirkgordon had to turn away as his face exploded into a silent laugh. He knew Austerley's eyes would be boring into the back of his head but this was priceless.

"Right then, Indy, better get you down to your room." Graham strode to the nearest hallway and shouted, "Clivey, are you down that way? Can you do me a delivery?" A gruff voice answered in the affirmative.

"Clivey" turned out to be a six-foot, broad-shouldered man of about thirty with a shaved complexion. Wiry black hair adorned his head and he seemed rather dour as he pushed Austerley towards his new room. After fetching some sticks, Graham escorted Kirkgordon to the room as well.

On hearing a bit of a commotion coming from Austerley's room (the reason for which seemed to be a debate on whether Austerley should have a particular copy of a book, whether or not it was in compact form), Kirkgordon made his excuses to Graham and wandered back along the corridor. Glancing into an open room, he saw an elderly lady sat on a bed staring at a mirror. She turned her head slowly and studied the stranger in the hall.

"Are you a policeman, son?" she enquired.

"No, madam, I'm not. Is there anything I can do for you?" asked Kirkgordon, feeling a yearning to be helpful.

"They did away with him. That's why I need a policeman. Not one of those constables either. Proper one like Morse or that French guy. Parrot."

"Poirot. He's Belgian."

"Sounds bloody French to me. Anyway, one of those ones. The ones who take care of the bodies." Well, thought Kirkgordon, Austerley's in the right place, this is indeed the nuthouse.

"Who's been done away with?"

"Norman Melville, of 4 Farnborough Road, Derbyshire. Pleasant man but a bit thick. Nasty habit of scratching his nuts too, when he sat down. Still, he didn't deserve that."

"Deserve what?"

"Getting killed. You really aren't a detective, are you? Too slow. Morse would be on to it by now."

"Who killed him? When?"

"Just this last week. And they did it. They come in the night if you've been chosen and take you away into the night. Then when you come back you're older. A lot older. I saw Norman before he went and when he came back he was at least forty years older." Kirkgordon raised his eyebrows. The lady was hunched with a protruding shoulder blade and she struggled to look up at him. He realized she was able to look comfortably in the mirror at him, though this gave the impression she wasn't interested in anything.

"Don't look at me like that son, bloody whippersnapper. I ain't mad. A little absent minded, but not mad. If you're marked they come for you and you gets old quick. From grape to raisin and a lot less hair," the old woman continued.

"So what happened to him?" She stayed silent, looking at the mirror, and Kirkgordon swore her eyes had glazed over. "I said, what happened to him?"

"There's no point talking to Massey, Churchy," said Graham from behind Kirkgordon. "She's catatonic. Lovely lady in her own way. Been here for three months now, little darling. But as far as conversation, she's not your girl. Awful pity."

Kirkgordon turned around to see if Graham's face matched his words but he saw no trace of any lie. But she had spoken alright. It was time to hold counsel, thought Kirkgordon, wait and see how things lie.

"Yes, Grahamsey, lovely woman."

"Indy is in a bit of a stushie and requesting your presence. Is he always this highly strung?"

"Well, you see, he's like a top-notch instrument. You have to know how to play him otherwise he just makes a dreadful racket."

Graham smiled and escorted Kirkgordon back to Austerley's room.

Standing on one foot beside the bed, Austerley was waving about a small book, out of the reach of a trim, petite blonde-haired girl who was dressed in blue scrubs. Her hair was tied back with a blue hairband, and from the rear she looked no more than eighteen. Clive was just leaving the room, shaking his head.

"What's the hassle, Indy?" asked Kirkgordon.

"This wench insists on taking my book from me, the Russian one! The ignorant cow thinks I'm liable to do myself an injury with it. Never heard such nonsense. It's my book, see, mine!"

He's such a petulant child at times, thought Kirkgordon. And being rude to a woman, too. Pretty little thing from behind.

And from the front too, it seems.

The girl had turned to face Kirkgordon and, although trim, had enough curves to show she had reached womanhood. Her face showed frustration, begging for help, and riding to her rescue came Sir Churchy Kirkgordon, vanquisher of all things Austerley.

"Just give her the book, Indy, and let's get on. I ain't had any tea."

"It's one of those books," countered Austerley. Ah, thought Kirkgordon, a little diplomacy required.

"Can I have a word, Miss? Grahamsey?" Once outside the room, Kirkgordon continued in a quiet voice. "Look, he's just a little embarrassed that you have found his stash." There were bewildered faces looking back. "His private reading." No change on the faces. Okay, delicate isn't working. "It's his porn. Okay? He's a bit embarrassed."

"But why is it called *Poems to raise the dead*?" asked the girl.

Arse, thought Kirkgordon, why does everyone read Russian except me? "It's just the cover. Quite clever, really. I mean, where do you hide yours?"

"Under-sink cupboard, in the bathroom." The last few words were said by Graham. There was an embarrassed silence as he realized he was speaking out loud.

"I'll just take it away, if that's agreeable?" concluded Kirkgordon. Graham walked away quickly, back up the corridor. The young girl nodded and looked into Kirkgordon's face.

"Are you going to be here long?" she asked.

"Two weeks, they say. I'm not staying here, but I'll be in town." Kirkgordon's eyes dropped from her face down to her chest. On the way they saw a necklace, made in a black metal with some intricate twists.

"Maybe I can show you around?"

"Well, I may need a guide." What's the harm, he thought. After all, it's not like I'm wanting to get her into bed. The girl returned to the room and Kirkgordon followed, taking the book from Austerley, saying he would hold it for him. The girl, on seeing that Austerley had everything he needed, left the room and Kirkgordon closed the door.

"You always take the side of the pretty girl. Your tongue was practically hanging out," accused Austerley.

"Hey, I got your book back. And don't have a go at me for window shopping. That's all it was."

"Well, I'm tired and my back's sore from you pulling me out of the train. I'm going to get some sleep." Kirkgordon threw the book at Austerley, hitting him in the midriff.

"There, but don't get caught with it. Had to tell them it was your naughty mag."

"Cheers for that. Labelled as a one-footed pervert already."

"I'll drop by tonight. Sleep well."

"Churchy, did you see it?"

"See what?" asked Kirkgordon, pissed off at being delayed.

"Her necklace." Kirkgordon gave Austerley a quizzical look. "Seen it before. Get me a picture of it if you can."

Kirkgordon nodded and waved goodbye in a dismissive fashion. Time for some quality freedom.

Stretching out his back, Kirkgordon braced himself for the walk back to the town centre, ready to search for a good restaurant. There was a shower just starting overhead but the lightness of the clouds said that it would be brief. As so often, the British weather was providing rain amidst strong sunshine. Just starting to walk, he heard a voice call him.

"Hey, before you go." He turned and saw the young nurse

again, still in her blue scrubs. "I finish at ten. Fancy picking me up and going for a pint? I can show you the good local ale. You don't look like an alcopop guy."

She's fast, thought Kirkgordon. He knew he shouldn't, but it would be late and not much alcohol would be involved. He reckoned he could trust himself.

"Okay, but it's not an all-nighter, okay? Just a pint or two."

"Quarter past ten. My car's here, so we can go straight from here." She turned to re-enter the building.

"One more thing." She turned around. "What's your name?"

"Titania, but everyone calls me Tania. Except Graham, he calls me Tansey." Kirkgordon laughed.

"Okay, Tania, see you then." He glanced at the necklace she wore before she turned. I'm just getting a photo, that's all. And some pleasant company. That's all. It's okay because that's all.

The Not-So-Honourable Captain Smith

The steak and ale pie at the King's Head pub was adequate but not a patch on Alana's cooking. Of all the things being back in her company had brought to the surface, one of the main ones was his appetite for her meals. Always thinking with my stomach: that's what my mother always said. Still, I sure could have eaten an Alana lasagne.

There were a couple of hours to kill until his rendezvous with Tania, and Kirkgordon's first thought was to spend them visiting Austerley. But they would be together for two weeks of this and they would probably be at each other's throats in no time. Stuff it, he thought, let's make the most of this free time. Despite being a Saturday evening, all Kirkgordon could find was an exhibition at the local arts centre.

The rotund and jolly lady on the desk gratefully accepted his two pounds for the "special" display and directed him towards a green door with flaking paint. "Smugglers and Bandits on the Dillingham Coast" read the A4 laminated sheet on the door. Classy, thought Kirkgordon. I'll bring Austerley here. At least if he wrecks anything it won't cost the earth.

Opening the door, Kirkgordon was accosted by a man-sized pencil drawing on the wall beside him. In fairness, while it was obviously an amateur effort, it did give off an aura of terror.

In an imposing tri-cornered hat, an incredibly detailed long jacket with gleaming buttons, and pantaloons that reminded Kirkgordon of the seventies, the bearded scoundrel was pictured in mid swing of a cutlass. Captain Tobias Smith was the slightly disappointing legend to the picture.

"Quite the man, was Captain Smith."

Kirkgordon turned around and found that the lady from the desk had appeared behind him.

"Sorry, didn't mean to frighten you."

"It's okay," said Kirkgordon, "I was just checking out this rather good portrait. Quite the pirate, this fellow."

"Well, thank you. It's one of mine," the lady answered and smiled. "I'm Jane Goodritch. I run the centre with what little funding we receive. You'd think someone didn't want the history of this town to be known."

"Oh, why's that?"

"Oh, it doesn't matter, just some local politics I guess. But you're not here for that, Mr...?"

"Kirkgordon." The lady waited for a first name. "Just Kirkgordon."

"Well, Kirk, the man in front of you has probably provided this town with the darkest hours ever known in its history. Captain Smith was a pirate, or a privateer if you prefer, who came home expecting to run this town with his ill-gotten foreign gold. But a religious order had been set up in his twenty-year absence and the townsfolk refused to make him Mayor on his return, despite all the money he was offering. He was so disgusted that he refused to live in the town and instead resided with his men on his boat in the bay.

"Then one night, without warning, he took his men ashore to sack the village. There was a night of chaos and most of the buildings burned. The town militia triumphed, but only barely."

"Sounds like a nasty case," commented Kirkgordon.

"That's not the end of the tale, Kirk," continued Jane, "not by a long chalk. You see, as Captain Smith was dying, he was asked by the local priest to confess his sins and receive redemption. Instead he swore a curse on the town, crying out to the devil, vowing that one day his kin would once again lay siege to the town and take it for their own."

"Well, bit of an 'in your face' to the priest then. I'm sure that went down well," chortled Kirkgordon.

"It's no laughing matter, Kirk. The man was serious. So much so that the authorities took his still-alive body, placed it in a cage and hung him right up on the hill where the crows used to gather. A warning to all who would dare to speak such things again. Over the weeks he starved to death and was pecked at by the birds. But then the body disappeared."

"So some of his cronies nabbed the body. Not a difficult trick."

"No, Kirk, it wasn't stolen – there was an armed guard. It just vanished. They say the devil took him at his word and has kept his body to one day deliver vengeance on the town." Jane Goodritch looked over absent glasses at Kirkgordon.

"Yeah, but it's all ice cream and bracing sea breezes these days. None of that nonsense. No witchcraft or devilry here. Is there?"

"Keep your eyes alert, Kirk. My eyes are always alert." Jane shuffled off back to her desk at the building's entrance, leaving Kirkgordon to ponder her words. With little else to do, Kirkgordon continued to look at the exhibits. All alluded to the story Jane had so vehemently described. Stories though, just stories, thought Kirkgordon. After all, if there was anything to it, old Havers would have had someone down here by now to sort it all out, wouldn't he?

On leaving the exhibition, Kirkgordon thanked Jane for her time and wished her a good night. He opened the door to the outside world but something was ringing in his mind. I should just leave it, it's just a dumb thought. Isn't it? Okay, just to clarify, I'll ask.

"Sorry, Jane, just one thing about that story of yours?"

"But of course, Kirk. How can I help?"

"When they hung him in the cage, overlooking the bay, where was it?"

"Ah, that. It's one of our scenic vantage points. You may have seen it on the town maps, the ones we give the tourists. Gibbet Point. Have you heard of it?"

"Yes. Yes, I have." Kirkgordon held in his head in a slight dip, a typical pose when he was thinking.

"Are you alright, Kirk?"

"Me? Oh, yes. Sorry, just pondering something. And thanks again. I do know the place."

"Okay then. Goodbye, Kirk."

"Goodnight, Jane. And it's Kirkgordon."

"What is?" But he was gone.

Austerley was avoiding "Grahamsey" as best he could. The damned man kept popping in every ten minutes just to make sure that "happy wee Indy" was okay. Despite Austerley recounting some of his wilder times with Calandra, his work colleague and former lover, the manager still seemed keen on him. If he didn't stop, Austerley was going to have to take action.

All this was distracting him from more important thoughts.

The necklace the young nurse had been wearing had seemed familiar but he was struggling to place it. Austerley racked his mind to recall where he had seen it before. It had definitely not been on a person but rather in a book he had been leafing through. But which one?

In his role as Professor of Occultic Affairs at Miskatonic University, Austerley had travelled to many libraries that are not well known. Or, at least, their special collections are known to only a few select scholars. It was one of these he had been in. Now, where was it? Austerley thought back, imagining himself sat at a reading table in the collections room. There was a design on the side of the table, some sort of shape. A triangle. Yes, a triangle. Nuts, too. And chocolate. Ah yes, Switzerland! He remembered the Rococo style, designed by Peter Thumb. It had been quite beautiful. Visualizing the book in front of him, he wrote the title on a scrap of paper. Certain books should not be mentioned out loud.

Austerley looked at the digital clock on the side table. Ten o'clock. Where the hell was Kirkgordon? He said he was going to drop in. The one time he might be of some use and he's not here. Austerley saw a bright flash of colour just outside his room.

"Graham?" Due to the pestering, Austerley was insistent on calling the manager by his proper name.

"Ah, Indy. Just checking you're settling in alright. Can't have our new guest left in any pickles, can we?"

"I'm fine. I was fine. I will be fine. Just bloody well leave me alone and give me some peace."

"Right you are, Indy. I'm just up the corridor if you need me."

Austerley looked at the scrap of paper with the book's title written on it. I wouldn't mind travelling to Switzerland myself. If it wasn't for this foot – or, rather, the lack of it. He looked up and saw a figure entering the room. "Kirkgordon," he swore out loud.

"I've just got here and you're in that tone already. What's up? Grahamsey not saying hello?" said Kirkgordon, breezing into the room.

"About bloody time. Where have you been?"

"Giving you space, so don't complain or I'll sit beside you all day."

"You need to phone Havers." Kirkgordon raised his eyebrows. "I need a book. It's in the Abbey Library of Saint Gall. Havers should know it. I've written the title down."

Kirkgordon read the title. "Is that Dutch?"

"No. It's not any language you'll know. But Havers will know what it is. Don't mention it to anyone else."

"Why? It's just a book."

"No it's not. There are some books you don't want to be advertising your fondness for. Just get hold of Havers and get me that book. Okay?"

"Sure thing. I'll get hold of him tomorrow."

"No!" shouted Austerley before dropping his voice. "Tonight. Do it now, with your phone or tablet or fax or something, but tonight! It's important."

"Okay. But I'm catching that nurse for a pint later, so it had better be quick."

"The nurse that was in here earlier?" asked Austerley.

"Yes, just a social drink. I'm not cradle snatching."

"Just be careful, Churchy. Be careful." With that, Austerley turned to the window.

Well, thought Kirkgordon, that was odd. He wandered back

out to the car park, returning a wave to Graham as he passed the front desk. Kirkgordon chortled to himself. *I bet he's got Austerley wound right up.*

The night was dry but fresh, and the trees made a brushing sound as several branches blew against each other. Looking inside the glass-fronted entrance, Kirkgordon could see Tania having an exchange with Graham. It seemed heated and he was shaking his head. She stormed out of the entrance, still dressed in her blue scrubs, with her jacket in her left hand. The wind blew her scrubs tight in a pleasing fashion, showing off her figure. *Just a pint,* Kirkgordon reminded himself.

"Sorry, I'm a wee bit late. Didn't have time to change, so I thought I'd just go like this, if that's okay," said Tania.

"I doubt you'd look bad in anything." Kirkgordon died inside. *How cheesy was that? It sounded like he was hitting on her. Not a great start.*

Tania dipped her head, as if in a blush, before extending her arm for Kirkgordon to take. "My car's over there. Probably best we take it as it's close to closing time," she suggested. Kirkgordon escorted her to a Renault Clio, deep red with a black interior. Hanging from the mirror were little skeletons and skulls, plastic and cheap, giving the effect of a Halloween stall.

"You like death, do you?" asked Kirkgordon, settling into the passenger seat.

"They're just little knick-knacks, that's all. I'm a nurse. Death is all around me."

"Bit morbid, at your age."

"Just honest." Tania turned the ignition and reversed before driving out of the car park. "It's just all the ideas and legends around death I like. Some of them are pretty cool." She smiled at Kirkgordon, who returned the grin and then found himself continuing to stare at her while she focused on the road. Just a pint, remember, just a pint.

"Austerley's your man, anyway. He knows all those legends. Bit of an expert on them," said Kirkgordon.

"Really? He just seems like a grumpy old fool."

"He's just worried about your manager. He thinks he's after him." Tania burst out laughing. "What? It doesn't seem that infeasible."

"You guys need to get with the twenty-first century. Graham isn't gay. He's just very colourful."

"You mean camp."

"Okay, yes, camp. But trust me, he's not into guys. In fact, the reason he was arguing with me was to try to get me to work overtime tonight."

"What's that got to do with it?" asked Kirkgordon.

"Well, he knew I was seeing you for a drink. He was trying to eliminate the competition. But don't worry," Tania said, stroking Kirkgordon's thigh, "I put him in his place. I've already got my admirer for the evening."

Man, she's forward, thought Kirkgordon. "I said one drink."

"We'll see." Her hand was still on his thigh.

Tania

You had to hand it to the English, their bitter was blooming good! Kirkgordon finished the third pint and sat back happily on the stool, looking at the young woman in front of him. She was matching him drink for drink but her stature meant the alcohol was having a greater effect on her. There was something carefree in her ways that really struck a chord with Kirkgordon. She seemed unfettered by the troubles he always carried with him.

"Tania, I think the barman's getting a bit pissed off with us. He's got the brush out and everything."

"Well, let's go on somewhere else. I'm not on until two or three tomorrow. Let's go have some fun," said Tania, grabbing Kirkgordon's hand before he could offer an answer. Kirkgordon left a fiver tip on the table for keeping the barman from his early finish. The bar had been empty except for the two of them, and having announced they were only there for a quick one, Kirkgordon felt guilty at keeping the tired-looking barman back.

The next half hour was spent walking the town looking for another bar, but all were closed for the night. Tania pointed out the gentleman's club that was open until 3 am but Kirkgordon didn't go to those places as a rule and certainly felt he already had enough to deal with in the shape of his companion.

"Maybe we should call it a night, Tania. It's one in the morning and I'm knackered."

"Time for a walk to wake you up, then. Look – the moon's coming out from the clouds. I know just the place. Let's go." She smacked his backside cheekily and ran off. Just a walk, thought Kirkgordon, it's just a walk.

The walk turned into a hike up a familiar hill. In the dark the place seemed to have more foreboding, but Gibbet Point was lit up postcard-fashion by the moon, which also set the water of the bay shimmering. Tania sat down on the grass overlooking the bay and tapped the ground for Kirkgordon to join her. He did so, leaving a small gap between them which Tania quickly closed. As she looked up into his face, Kirkgordon noticed the necklace with the symbol Austerley had mentioned. His partner's warning came back to him.

"Do you know what this place is?" asked Tania.

"Actually I do. 'Cause I'm a regular history guru."

"Go on then, Mr Schama, tell me all," laughed Tania.

"Well, there was this pirate fella who thought he should run the place after coming back from plundering afield. However, the locals said 'No way, Jose' and he attacked them. Lots of people died and he was taken but made a pact with the devil for revenge. Have I got it straight?"

Tania laughed. "Someone tell Mr Schama his job is safe!" Reaching up behind his head, she stroked his neck gently. "You seem to have missed out the love aspect."

"Oh. Power, greed, slaughter and devil worship but there's a love interest? Sounds intriguing."

"Listen, Mr Sceptical. There's more romance in this dead pirate than there is in you."

"Go on then, prove it."

"Well," said Tania, "when he came back from his travels, he had a wife from the Caribbean. They said she was a black beauty with eyes of fire and long dark flowing curls. Some said she was over a hundred years old but had made a deal with the Evil One to keep her youth. She was full of black magic and power, capable of seducing anyone in her path. One of the reasons the townsfolk didn't like Captain Smith returning was that his new bride would dance on board the deck of the ship in full view of the town."

"That seems to be a bit much, being against someone for dancing. There was film back in the eighties where a whole town was against dancing but this young lad took some of the other young people across the state border and—"

"It wasn't the dancing. You are such an idiot. And how am I going to know about some eighties film?"

"It's a very good film, actually."

"I don't care," laughed Tania. "Listen, when she danced, she danced naked, sacrificing animals."

"Ah, now that's just unsociable."

"Oi!" Tania elbowed Kirkgordon in the ribs. "Shut up and listen."

"Listening, ma'am." Kirkgordon rubbed some sore ribs.

"Good. Now, the townsfolk, on seeing this, grabbed her one night and burned her as a witch. The ashes sank into the ground after some heavy rain and they say her soul still inhabits the area. That was why he attacked the village. They took his love and so he demanded revenge."

"Tania, I have to be honest and say never write a romance book, 'cause it isn't going to sell," laughed Kirkgordon. She dived at him, knocked him to the ground and clambered on top.

"Let's have some fun," said Tania.

"This is fun."

"No, real fun. Fancy a skinny dip?"

Part of Kirkgordon screamed yes but another part knew this was crazy – not the actions of a man trying to get back with his wife. Caught in two minds, he prayed for an escape. He felt his phone vibrating. "My phone's buzzing, Tania. Sorry, at this time of night I really need to check it. It must be important."

Sighing, Tania rolled off. "Probably just an update for your calendar," she muttered.

Kirkgordon pressed the screen on and saw a text message: Mr Austerley in hysterics. Please come. Come quick.

"Tania, it's Indy. Sounds like he's wrecking the joint. I need to get back to the care home."

"I'll come with you."

"There's no need. I can cope."

"Hey, he's my patient too." She took Kirkgordon by the hand and started to race down the hill. As they made their way back down the hill, Kirkgordon wondered how he got himself into these positions. Why do I let myself get so close to the fire? I tell Austerley to back off the occult but I keep getting dragged in by women. Although Alana would question the word "dragged".

Racing into the town, they found a taxi to take them to the care home. The drive was short but Kirkgordon noticed that Tania insisted on holding his hand. He made sure they parted hands on leaving the taxi. There were lights on in the entrance and Graham was in a panic at the front desk.

"Mr Kirkgordon! Good, I was just about to call the police. He's very violent. Got the whole place awake."

"Ah, bollocks," said Kirkgordon. He recognized the results of an Austerley nightmare. Having babysat him for over a month now, he was used to the reactions. However, they had been less frequent recently and Kirkgordon had hoped they were gone.

He tore down the corridor, Tania racing behind with Graham bringing up the rear in a loud chequered shirt. On entering Austerley's room, Kirkgordon saw Austerley, dressed in only a pair of boxers, on his single foot delivering a right hook to Clive's jaw.

"Enough!" shouted Kirkgordon and strode forward, picking Austerley up by the throat and driving him back to the bed. He stared into Austerley's eyes and shouted, "You're not in trouble. It's safe. No dragons. Farthington is not here. He's gone, Austerley. Gone! Calm down. Calm! Now! Calm."

Austerley's eyes were wide and uncomprehending but under Kirkgordon's influence he started to unwind. Gradually he looked around, assuring himself of his location. Finally at peace, he stared at the others in the room.

"What the hell do they want?" asked Austerley.

"Everyone leave, please," ordered Kirkgordon. "Just leave. You too, Tania, thanks. Everyone, thank you, just leave and close the door. It's okay, I have this." When he was sure everyone had left, Kirkgordon turned to face Austerley again and released the grip on his throat. "You okay?"

"Bloody magic. Give me my dressing gown. And some water too."

"Yes, your majesty," whispered Kirkgordon to himself and turned to retrieve the items. Once Austerley was dressed and sitting up, Kirkgordon started the questioning.

"Was it Farthington again?" Farthington was the dragon that had ripped off Austerley's foot. The incident had left Austerley with recurrent nightmares.

"Yes. Well, mostly."

"Mostly? Not all, then?"

Austerley shook his head.

"What else?"

"A cage. A round one, tall enough for a human. Swinging in the wind."

Kirkgordon nodded. It was best not to question why at this point, but to let Austerley recount the details in his own time.

"Do you remember that programme?" Austerley continued. "Dahl, the children's writer. His stories. Tales of something."

"The unexpected."

"Yes, that's it. But not any of the stories. Just the start. I can see the start of it."

As Kirkgordon recalled, the start was a woman dancing in silhouette with not much on.

"That it?"

"I think so. Are there any sleeping tablets?" asked Austerley.

"Yeah." Kirkgordon searched in Austerley's belongings and threw him some tablets.

"That's a double dose."

"Yeah," answered Kirkgordon.

Austerley dropped the tablets with a glass of water and lay down on the bed. Taking a chair in the corner of the room, Kirkgordon watched his partner fall asleep. He knew not to fall asleep himself or he would end up waking in the chair, sore and groggy, in a couple of hours. As he watched Austerley drop into a deep sleep, the wounded leg seemed to stare at Kirkgordon. He had seen amputees before, in Sierra Leone when he had worked for a client, but this was a wound he had caused. The stump was just there, reminding him of that fateful arrow, his arrow, pinning Austerley to the platform that had collapsed. He could still see Farthington, the dragon, separating foot from leg with one of his three heads. And though Havers had told him on many occasions that Kirkgordon had done the right and necessary thing, it still didn't take the guilt away.

There was a knock at the door. It opened and Tania came into view. With a single finger, she beckoned Kirkgordon out of the room. He found it hard to deny that he enjoyed the intrusion.

"Just wondered if you wanted a more comfortable bed," whispered Tania.

She's certainly forward, thought Kirkgordon. "I really need to be near, Tania. It's just that he often gets reoccurrences. It wouldn't be doing to be otherwise occupied when one of the dreams come. He had been a week without an episode but this last one wasn't so good."

Tania was smiling up at him. "I wasn't offering any sporting activities. There's a rest room, for the nurses, with beds. Just thought it might be more comfortable than that chair in there."

"Oh, sorry. I didn't mean to…"

"It's okay. It has been good. And I like you a lot for an oldie, but it takes a while before I climb into bed with someone. But don't panic. You're still on the possible list." She reached up and kissed his cheek before turning and walking away. He looked her up and down, thinking how much he liked scrubs, before realizing how close he had been to falling into Tania's arms.

It doesn't do to be too far from Alana, thought Kirkgordon.

To avoid the awkward subject of his own failings as a husband and father, he ran through the things he still had to do in Dillingham. Oh yes, contact Havers for Austerley to get that book. Still, I can do that in the morning. No, sod it, let's wake the bugger up. After all, he's always manipulating us.

Courage failed Kirkgordon and he ended up walking to the

car park to send a text to Havers instead. The night air was cold now as it was shortly about to catch the morning, and Kirkgordon found it refreshing. For a few moments he closed his eyes, listened to the quiet rustling of the few creatures on the move and took in the breeze tingling his wet lips. Some sort of paradise, he thought. Then his mobile phone vibrated.

"It's 4 am, who the hell's this?" asked Kirkgordon to the disturber of his peace.

"Ah, Mr Kirkgordon. Good to see you are not resting on your laurels. Major Havers speaking and, as I recall, you are the one who sent me a text message requesting a certain item."

"Do you sleep, Havers?"

"Do you, Mr Kirkgordon?"

"Okay, touché."

"Please tell Mr Austerley I shall obtain his book at once and deliver it to him by the fastest possible method. Do tell me, Mr Kirkgordon, is Mr Austerley faring well?"

"Well, he's just had one of the attacks, Havers. Quite bad by recent standards, too. Actually smacked one of the nurses."

"What was the subject of the nightmare?"

"Usual suspect. Farthington ripping his foot off and that. But there were a few new elements. A swinging cage and some nude dancing chick in silhouette."

"Anything else?" Havers sounded worried.

"No. Expecting extras, were you?"

"Keep your wits about you, Mr Kirkgordon. Mr Austerley is, as you know, receptive. New dreams always give cause for concern. But I shall depart now as I have a plane to catch." There was a whirring sound in the background, loud like a fierce wind.

"Are you on a plane?"

"Not quite yet, Mr Kirkgordon, but my library books are overdue. Be vigilant." And the line went dead.

Aw, crap, thought Kirkgordon, Havers never says things in jest. I'm tired, at the dry end of a few pints and about to babysit the mad end of an occult receiver. The only positive thing is a young girl who says I'm on her "to bed" list. And that's a positive I really need to avoid. I just love my job.

Father Jonah

It might seem strange to some people, thought Kirkgordon, but I need to go to church today. He remembered the look Austerley had given him and the snide comment about Tania as he had left the room. I probably deserved that one. Why did people always think you had to be perfect to go to church? Anyway, that's up to them, not me. Kirkgordon knew his God had been there on that island even though the events hadn't been pleasant.

The morning was bright and fresh after a little clearing rain and the birdsong complemented the smell of the oak trees, their leaves dripping. The sun was still cool, and Kirkgordon felt refreshed as he walked. Tired, oh yes, very tired, but refreshed. His mind wandered back to a day the previous week when he had been holding his son in his arms before letting him loose on the public play park, and he wondered why it couldn't be like that all the time. His son didn't know his Dad fought with demons from parts of the skies unseen by human eyes. And, thankfully, the boy had never met Austerley.

St Jude's was a modest grey building. It had the obligatory steeple but also a modern building attached at the side. Although this building was dark now, Kirkgordon could see tables, chairs and a large sign telling folks to "come on in for rest, prayer and a fill-up". Come to think of it, he could do with a decent meal. He hadn't had any breakfast and last night's beer had left him hungry. But 9:30 am for a service? Day of rest, wasn't it?

After shaking hands with an elderly gentleman in the entrance vestibule, Kirkgordon took a prayer book and hymnal and sat down three rows from the back. There were in the region of thirty other people there. A greying priest, in quite reserved garb for an Anglican, emerged from the rear along with a posse containing three choirboys and a junior. The priest, who was a good six inches smaller than Kirkgordon, nodded knowingly as he passed by. As the priest reached the front of the main aisle, another man sat down beside Kirkgordon.

Kirkgordon buckled at the smell coming from the man. I know that smell, thought Kirkgordon. That's horse shit, genuine manure. Wearing a dirty, blackened overcoat and worn-through jeans, the man – Kirkgordon assumed he was a tramp – coughed loudly. Some of the spittle landed on Kirkgordon's knee. The tramp placed a yellow plastic bag on the floor and proceeded to pick his nose with total abandon. Out of the corner of his eye, Kirkgordon could see a matted beard and missing teeth. And eyes that resonated wariness.

After a moment, Kirkgordon realized that the eyes were out of place. Damn he's good, thought Kirkgordon. I'm six inches off his face or I wouldn't have got it. Total pro, he's a total pro. But if he's here, we are really in trouble.

"Is that his book?" whispered Kirkgordon.

The tramp nodded gently.

"You smell like crap."

"The manure is genuine, Mr Kirkgordon. You are being watched, so don't pick up the book. I'll leave it behind for the priest to find. Make sure you stop and chat with him today. They're pretty modern for Anglicans, here. Coffee and doughnuts after the service." The tramp – or, more correctly, Austerley and Kirkgordon's boss, Havers – spoke in barely audible tones. Every now and then he would break into a deep, chesty cough and spit on the ground. It certainly gave the pair of them a great deal of room.

Havers stayed for the whole church service, playing the part of the tramp incredibly well. On leaving, he even managed to fall into the arms of a rather snooty lady with a large bonnet. Kirkgordon chuckled to himself as he watched her try to appear Christian, feigning help for the tramp while keeping as great a distance as possible. Having taken a moment to let Havers leave, Kirkgordon was the last person to exit the nave and shake hands with the priest.

"Thank you, vicar, nice service," ventured Kirkgordon.

"Why, thank you Mr...?" asked the priest.

"Kirkgordon. All one word. All one surname. Seems to cause some confusion round here."

"Scottish name, you see. Not used to that sort of name round here. Bit too far south." The priest's voice was laboured, like he was struggling with the delivery of the words rather than the thought processes. His eyes looked glassy, roaming without ever finding a target, almost as if they were redundant while his mind worked on weightier things.

"Well, I'm not from round here. Just babysitting a friend at the care home."

"Oh dear, is your friend alright?" asked the priest.

How do I put this, thought Kirkgordon? He's about to get a prosthetic because I shot him in the foot with an arrow while trying to kill him to prevent him from summoning a demon and then a three-headed dragon ripped his ankle apart. "He's getting a new foot after a serious accident," he said.

"Sorry to hear that. I'm Father Jonah, Mr Kirkgordon, but I'm often known as *olhos dos outros* to my friends. Ohlos for short. But where are my manners? Come back to the manse for dinner. My daughter is an excellent cook. I bet you enjoy mussels, Mr Kirkgordon."

Kirkgordon knew that he was to receive the book from the priest but as nothing was forthcoming yet he decided he had better stick close. Besides, it gave him an excuse to be away from Austerley.

After retiring for a short time, Father Jonah returned, dressed in a white monk's habit complete with cord belt. The old man must have clocked Kirkgordon's strange looks because he explained that he had been a monk before God had led him into service with this particular church.

"Just as all my troubles seemed to have reached a head, I was finally able to see the way," he said.

Kirkgordon nodded politely but was feeling a little uncomfortable. This was one rather kooky individual.

Leading Kirkgordon to the back of the church, Father Jonah pointed to a red motorcycle, announcing it as their mode of transport. He threw over a helmet with a cross motif on it. Over the priest's habit he threw on a motorcycle jacket displaying a message of the grace of heaven. Kirkgordon felt he was riding with the holiest of Hell's Angels except for the strict adherence to the speed limit. It was not long before he recognized the route.

The care home came into sight and the priest rode easily into the car park, stopping right in front of the main entrance. Without a word, he reached inside his habit and handed Kirkgordon the yellow packet Havers had left behind.

Kirkgordon wasted no time in taking the book to Austerley. He advised Austerley not to get his crayons on it and received an expletive in reply. On Kirkgordon's return to the motorcycle, Father Jonah said nothing but drove back to the church, parking in the same spot.

"I guess lunch is off the menu, then. Well, thanks for the book." Kirkgordon turned to go.

"My house is the one beside the church. You need to talk and there are many questions you need answered. But first we eat the mussels."

The priest walked off leaving Kirkgordon stunned. How did he know so much about him? And so accurate. It took all his composure not to yell at this crazy man. Kirkgordon followed him into the house.

A young girl, possibly twelve or thirteen, took Kirkgordon's coat before scuttling back to what was presumably the kitchen. The priest led his guest into a bland sitting room with an old sofa. The cover reminded Kirkgordon of a seventies convention – he swore it should be wearing flares. There was a wooden table on which was a single bottle of supermarket sherry and two large tumblers. The priest poured two generous measures and handed a tumbler to Kirkgordon.

These are no sherry glasses, he thought. And he's no priest.

Father Jonah waved Kirkgordon towards the sofa. The girl brought in a plate of mussels with a small fork and handed it to their guest. After blessing the food, the priest motioned for Kirkgordon to eat and they sat in silence.

Kirkgordon barely managed to avoid spitting out his food as he realized the mussels were pickled. What on earth is this nonsense, he thought. His tongue railed at the sharp, acidic taste and part of him just wanted his bed.

But Kirkgordon had been raised on good manners and he managed to finish his plate. The girl came back so quickly for the cleared dish that he was sure she had been watching from somewhere. The priest remained mute and produced a plastic tub with some small holes in its lid. Opening the receptacle carefully, he took out a toad and walked towards Kirkgordon. Without warning, the man placed the toad on Kirkgordon's head and retreated to a distance of about five feet.

This is surreal, just crackers, thought Kirkgordon. Where does Havers get these clowns? Still, I had better see it through. No doubt there will be some strange spiritual significance. There had better be!

Looking straight at Kirkgordon, the priest began to spit at him, drawing up huge amounts of snot through his nose. Several globules landed on Kirkgordon's clothes before two caught him square on the face. That's it! That is damn well it, thought Kirkgordon.

"Right, you'd better have a damn good reason for this, vicar. I've never smacked a holy man before but you're going to be the first unless you come up with a good excuse. And fast, too!" raged Kirkgordon.

"Ah, good. So, you are not just one of Havers' pigeons, then. Sitting there, doing what they are told. That's good, really good."

"What are you on about? Are you saying this was some sort of a test? There are other ways. And get me a bloody towel. Gobbing on people is disgusting."

"Havers' last man, Wilson, was a true devotee. Sat right through everything I did and never complained once. Nothing to upset the contact. Poor boy. Excuse my language, but Havers is a bastard, a slave to the job. He doesn't care one jot for his people." The girl returned to the room and handed Kirkgordon a small towel to wipe himself down.

"I'm a little confused. This was all to see if I was one of Havers' men? I guess he pays the bills, so I am. And he isn't totally cold, he just puts the job first."

"In the stakes of a holy war, people often get neglected or eliminated as a problem, sir. But a holy war is all about people."

"Holy war? What are you on about? Evangelism?" asked Kirkgordon.

"No. The war that is coming. Why are you here, Mr Kirkgordon? Why?"

"Well, Austerley has this problem with his foot. Actually, with having no foot. On that leg." Kirkgordon tapped his leg.

"His foot is as much your problem as his. But that's not why you are here. Havers did not need you to be a nurse."

"Wilson. You said the previous guy was Wilson. Where is Wilson?" asked Kirkgordon.

"Gone. Missing. Disappeared. That's all I know, but Havers knows more. Havers always knows more."

"You can say that again."

"Now listen carefully, Mr Kirkgordon. When it happens—"

"When what happens?"

"When it happens, sir, he'll want you to destroy them all."

"Havers will?"

The priest nodded. "But remember mercy and restoration and forgiveness. Remember them well."

"Why? And for who?"

The priest turned and exited the room.

"Father is done now. Please take heed of what he says," said the girl.

"But what's coming?"

From behind her back, the girl produced a man's necklace with a solid dangling cross on it and handed it to Kirkgordon. "Here. So you remember. God bless." Then she opened the door that led out of the house.

Kirkgordon tried to speak but the girl didn't even look at him, she just held the door open. His time here was clearly finished. I want a normal life, he thought. And the next time someone gobs on me I will floor them. I don't care who they are.

Kirkgordon stepped back out to the church car park and started to walk back to the care home. His stomach rumbled so he detoured via the nearest pub for some lunch. Things were getting strange. I need Austerley, he thought. If I'm in the kingdom of madness then the crown prince should be able to furnish me with some details.

The Offensive Side of Havers

Something wasn't right, thought Kirkgordon. It might be Sunday afternoon and Austerley might have had a big lunch but there was no way he would be sleeping after having got his hands on that book. He had been so insistent about getting it and had really thought he was onto something. No, this would not do. Something was wrong.

Turning around, Kirkgordon left Austerley lying asleep in his room, snoring loudly on his bed. Kirkgordon needed answers and someone was going to have to explain what was going on. In his haste, he nearly knocked an old lady over. Standing in just a pink nightgown, she stared at Kirkgordon for a few seconds before grabbing him by the wrist.

"It's okay dear, I'll just get someone to help you," he told her. "Nurse! Little help required, nurse!" The old woman tugged hard at his arm. "Okay dear, what is it?" He noted the deep wrinkles on her skin. She was leathery, as if she had been soaked and then left to wrinkle in the sun. Kirkgordon reckoned she must have been close to a hundred.

For all her supposed age she seemed to have the strength of six good men. In fact, her nails were digging into Kirkgordon's arm but he ignored the pain and let her lead him. She stopped at a doorway and pointed inside. Looking in, Kirkgordon saw a gentleman of maybe fifty years lying asleep on his bed. He was covered up by a drab blue quilt and there was a glass of water by his beside. Also by the bed were some family photos, a Gideon's bible, a jug of water and a bottle of a golden energy drink. And one other object, which the old lady began to point at.

It was an emerald brooch encircled with diamonds and rusted clasps. It looked rather unremarkable to Kirkgordon but the lady was making a big fuss about it. Getting agitated at Kirkgordon's lack of interest, she pointed back and forth from the brooch to the sleeping gent.

"There, there, Mrs Moor. Are you after that brooch again?" It was Tania, complete in her scrubs.

Damn, she looks good in those, thought Kirkgordon.

"Sorry about this," said Tania, "but Mrs Moor has a thing about that brooch. Reckons it's hers. I'll just get her back to her bed."

"Thanks, Tania," said Kirkgordon, his gaze dwelling just a little too long on her tight-fitting attire.

As Tania tried to lead Mrs Moor away, the old lady grabbed Kirkgordon's arm again and held on so tightly that her nails drew blood. As her grip eventually slackened her eyes went wild and she blurted out, "I used to have life. I had my life. Now they have it. They have it."

"Yes, Mrs Moor, us young ones certainly are having our day aren't we?" Tania chirped in quickly and hurried her out of the room.

There's something attractive about a caring woman, thought Kirkgordon. He told himself he was just watching Tania help the old lady, appreciating her professional vocation, but when his mind conjured up the image of a thong, Kirkgordon realized his old habits were surfacing all too readily.

Feeling a bit stuck for action, Kirkgordon hovered by the room entrance, hoping Tania would return. After five minutes he recognized her scrubs coming back around the corner. Her smiling face sent a pleasing wobble into his stomach and he began to beam.

"Sorry about that. Mrs Moor is a bit mad on other people's things. Always reckons they belong to her, from her dodgy past, no doubt. Poor old dear," said Tania.

"Is she okay?" asked Kirkgordon.

"Yes, she's fine. I enjoyed last night by the way." Kirkgordon felt Tania take his hand. She rubbed it gently on the outside with her thumb. "Was a shame to have ended it that way. I would have preferred to have shown you the sunrise."

"I'm sure the view would have been great."

"It would have been. My flat's got a small balcony, very secluded. And the sun shines right into it as it breaks the horizon. There's nothing like the feel of the first rays chasing the cool night from your bare skin."

Kirkgordon felt slightly weak. That's just unfair, he thought. Totally horny, but unfair.

"Next time," said Tania, "next time." She held his gaze and noticed his jaw drop slightly as he glanced at her necklace. She leaned forward slightly. "I don't think it's my necklace you're wanting to look at," teased Tania.

Actually, thought Kirkgordon, it is. Why have I got Austerley's mad ramblings racing through my head at a moment like this? Damn him.

"What happened to Austerley? He's sleeping like a log," said Kirkgordon, to break the moment.

"Oh, your friend," chirped Tania, reverting to a more upright pose. "They had to sedate him. For his own good, the notes said. Apparently he was getting into a right state so they decided his body needed a rest."

"Why wasn't I informed? The arrangements were that I was to be notified if he started to get agitated again."

"I guess they knew you were out last night and decided to let you sleep. Pretty decent of them, really."

"Maybe so, but I need to know all his issues when they happen. Can you reiterate that to them?"

"Of course. But I suggest they keep him sedated tonight."

"Why?"

"You don't want to miss the sunrise." Tania turned away almost skipping, letting her long hair bounce freely.

Such a tease, thought Kirkgordon but then corrected himself. A tease would be fine. A little excitement but no real chance of doing anything I shouldn't. No, she's playing for keeps. That's not fair. He tried to focus on Alana but her hair got interchanged with Tania's and then the faces blurred. In fact, every time he tried to think of a deep, loving moment with Alana, Tania's face and body would appear in that moment. I need a shrink, he thought. Or a good crack across the skull.

Stumbling slightly, Kirkgordon managed to get himself to the front door before falling to his knees outside. He drew in the salt air in deep mouthfuls but the nauseous state persisted. He decided to walk back to his accommodation. Maybe I have just been up too long, he thought.

Over the next hour he pitched haphazardly, but on a reasonably direct route, to the front door of his guest house. On seeing the state he was in, the lady of the house took him by the hand and helped deposit him into his room. Kirkgordon managed to undress himself and clamber into bed. He closed his eyes.

Tania was beside him. And the sun was rising.

When you needed privacy, Havers found the best way to clear an area was to be as offensive as possible without speaking. So he wasn't dressed in his usual crisp suit and bowler hat but instead continued with his tramp disguise. On reaching the viewpoint known as Gibbet Point, he had observed a number of couples and individuals enjoying the day. The scene was calm and peaceful and he felt slight remorse at ruining Sunday afternoon for these good people. But this was where the signal had come from. The tech crew had confirmed it and now he needed to work the scene.

Sidling up to one couple, he sat down beside them without a word. The reaction was instantaneous.

"Bloody hell, brother, get a bath!"

Soon the area was almost clear. Genuine manure always worked well. The stupid tramp, sleeping in the wrong field. But then he struck a problem. The last remaining person, an older lady on her own, actually undid her flask and handed him a cup of tea. Havers took it and spat the tea into the air.

Undaunted, the lady started asking questions. Did he have accommodation? Did he know where he could get help? Had he been homeless for long? These types were the hardest, thought Havers. Caring people are the hardest to move.

But then the woman left in a hurry. Someone urinating at her feet was just too much. Who knows what a man like that could do next? She was a woman alone, after all. He'd already cleared everyone else away. As she sped down the hill, she tried to dislodge the image from her head.

Havers, having adjusted himself back to decency, began to bring out some devices from under his coat. He wasn't entirely sure how they worked. That is to say, he could operate them but he didn't know why they functioned like they did. In his job, science, magic and the paranormal world all blended and you had to be beyond yourself to understand it all. But Havers was the controller so he couldn't go there. He needed a dispassionate, cool and untainted head. Keeping his delvers-into-the-strange-happenings close meant he had access to all the tools without the risk of attachment.

A grey box with a whirling antenna began to beep. A black stone on the ground changed to a purple tint. And a small mirror, over which Havers had watched a colleague recite an unknown incantation, showed a green outline, shimmering. Confirmed, then. Something was being brought here.

Havers quickly gathered the objects back into the concealed pockets of his coat. He needed to find out who was doing this. Wilson hadn't sent back much information and the initial comments from the priest had hardly been conclusive. A "strange evil presence" wasn't much to go on. If he hadn't known Father Jonah personally, he wouldn't even have sent Wilson. Havers stumbled like a drunk across the area, looking for anything else of note.

There was blood on that grass. Old, certainly. But blood. Reaching down, he plucked a few blades of the grass from the ground. His other hand reached inside his coat and pulled out a tiny black box. He opened a small drawer and placed the grass inside. Scratching his ear, he opened up the communications link with headquarters.

"Caretaker here," came the response from his earpiece. "*Alpha four X-ray papa niner seven two delta Charlie.*"

"Prime. *Romeo Fife tree Juliet foxtrot Lima wun ait niner sierra.* Sample in for analysis. Is it his?" Havers wandered over to the lookout point. There had been no further contact from Wilson.

He had sent a panic distress signal and then disappeared. It didn't look good.

They all assumed he didn't feel anything. Mr Cold, the Iceman, they called him. The one who would always do what was necessary, even if that meant killing one of his own. And he would. He knew that. But it didn't mean he liked it or that he didn't think about it. I lose a bit of my soul every day in this job, he thought. Wilson might be better off having not climbed the ladder. Even dead, he probably still was. Still, it won't comfort his parents. George and Anthea. Their only son, too.

"Prime?" asked his earpiece.

"Here," answered Havers.

"Affirmative."

"Prime changing to aggressive observation. Alert the stand-bys. This looks like trouble."

"Roger."

Havers looked out to the sea. His intuition was screaming at him but he wasn't sure what it was saying. Perhaps the priest could help. And Austerley might know. He was a receiver, after all. Austerley always received dreams or visions when there were supernatural or occult happenings afoot. An enormous sense of dread came over Havers as he looked out to the sea. Time to find out more about the history of this place, he thought.

Delivery and Collections

A parcel van pulled up outside the care home, much to the surprise of Graham. He had worked as the manager for over a year and no delivery had ever happened on a Sunday. Especially not a Sunday evening. Still, he thought, I'm here working so why not anyone else?

A uniformed driver stepped out of the van, entered the building and approached Graham at the front desk. "Hello. It's been a heck of a day, sorry it's a bit late," said the driver.

"It's fine. Sunday working, always a joy to do. I understand perfectly."

"I'm looking for a Mr Austerley. Have a special delivery for him which needs to be delivered in person."

"Ah," answered Graham. "That could be a problem. Mr Austerley is not in a fit condition to sign anything."

"Oh. Well, do you mind if I take this up to his room? It's a celebration package and I've been instructed to set it up for him. Shouldn't take too long."

"Well, Mr...?"

"Gavin, call me Gavin."

"Gavin. Well now, Gavin, that could be awkward. We're a little low on staff at the moment and I can't really leave the front desk," said Graham.

"I get what you're saying, governor, but it's quite a special thing, this. Especially for people about to go to hospital. That's what it says, anyway. Just a wee balloon thing. Do you mind? I'll go there myself and that. If you don't mind."

Graham thought for a moment. Then he broke into a large smile.

"Look, okay. Just because of what it is. Mind you don't hang about. Also, if Mr Austerley wakes up, don't speak to him or anything, just come and get me. He can be a wee bit temperamental. That's one disease that can't be cured, unfortunately."

"Sure, governor. Not a moment too long up there, I gotcha. Where is it?"

Graham gave the directions to follow and the delivery man strolled calmly away, holding the large box under his arm. Good, thought Havers, I'll get to see him alone. This disguise is pretty effective.

Havers could hear Austerley's snoring from outside the door. In fairness, he had heard him a corridor away but hadn't realized who it was. The room he entered looked neat and tidy. Austerley was lying on the bed under a duvet. Shutting the door gently behind him, Havers got out a torch and opened one of Austerley's eyelids. He tapped Austerley's forearm and slapped his face gently. Dammit, he thought, they must have given him enough to knock out a rhino.

There was a noise in the corridor. Havers broke open the box and took out a jaunty balloon which had emblazoned on it "Make sure to get a good footing". He was crouching down to fix the balloon to its stand when the door opened and a young woman dressed in scrubs entered.

"Is everything alright? Graham said you would be here. I just wanted to make sure Mr Austerley wasn't disturbing you," said the woman.

"Oh, no, not a word from him. Plenty of snoring, mind."

"It's a bit sick that, really."

"The balloon? It's a personal message so maybe he's a bit sick too. You see all sorts doing this."

"I suppose. Is that you finished? Doesn't look like much to it."

"Yes, that's me. Just going to grab my things." Havers spotted a book on the table beside Austerley's bed. The same one he had handed to Kirkgordon that morning. Now, he thought, that can't be lying around for all sorts to read. Careless, guys, careless. He picked up his box and turned around, shielding the book behind him. "Time to go, I guess." As he spoke, Havers' free hand picked the book off the table and held it to his back as he walked away. "You first, ma'am." As the young woman exited he brought the book round quickly and dropped it into his box.

Havers felt the woman's eyes on his back all the way down the corridor and was careful to stay in character. "Thanks for your time, mate," he said to Graham as he reached the front desk. "Cracking body on that nurse of yours." Graham nodded and Havers walked out of the building with his contraband.

Havers sat in the van and tried to visualize the scene he had been in. Something was up and he didn't believe Austerley's sedation was above board. Water jug, glass, all looked okay. Suitcase, yes, normal. The book being left out in the open wasn't so normal. Certainly not from Austerley. He would have understood the danger of what it contained. Kirkgordon? Maybe the error was his. Everything else looked fine, nothing out of place. Except... what was that small object close to the bed? His brain had registered it ever so briefly but there was definitely something unusual there. Closing his eyes, he drew the memory out of his mind. Small, it was small. A token perhaps? No. Slightly bigger. Green, definitely green. Emerald, there was an emerald. And diamonds. A brooch. That was it, a brooch. Better sketch it for the boys back at HQ.

Next stop was Mr Kirkgordon. Perhaps it was time to enlighten him about Wilson. Hopefully the priest had been of use to him. The trouble with Father Jonah was that he took some convincing. A good man, no doubt, but not always one to toe the line in service of the country. Or of those who protect it, at least.

The results from the lookout point were troubling Havers. The amount of background spiritual energy was alarming. Usually with results like that one would expect "disturbances", things the general public would have spotted. Nothing too outlandish, but certainly reportable. But he had checked with the police and there had been nothing unusual, nothing.

Havers tapped his ear and once HQ had checked in with the codes he asked them to find a local historian for him. The name came back. A Miss Jane Goodritch, working at the local arts centre. Havers decided that he would visit her after checking on Kirkgordon. He pulled up to the side of the road five hundred yards from Kirkgordon's guest house.

Checking the street as he approached the house, Havers noticed he was being watched from a red hatchback just opposite the guest house. Inside was a black-haired woman and a balding man who, on seeing him, began to kiss. Pretty amateurish, thought Havers. They are far too close to the building. I'd sack my people for a tail like that. As Havers reached the door, it opened, forcing him to take a step back. A rotund lady stepped out of the house.

"I'm sorry there's no answer from his door, Miss Goodritch, but I shall certainly tell him you called," said an older lady standing in the doorway.

"Miss Goodritch?" enquired Havers. "Miss Jane Goodritch?"

The rotund lady was taken aback. "Yes. Who's asking?"

"Allow me to introduce myself, ma'am. Major Havers. Arthur Lewis Siddlington-Havers, at your service."

"Very good, sir, and congratulations on such an impressive name, but why are you asking for me?"

"Dear lady, I think we have come to see the same person. Mr Kirkgordon."

"Kirk? You mean Mr Gordon. His first name's Kirk."

"As you wish. Is he well?"

"He's in his room asleep," said the landlady. "I was telling Miss Goodritch that he hasn't moved since he came in today. Sorry, but you'll have to come back."

"Ladies, forgive me, but kindly step back inside the building."

"Why should we?" asked Miss Goodritch.

"Because my gun says so. It has a silencer and I am capable of delivering the necessary blow if required but I'd be happier if you just got inside quickly. Before they really take an interest in you."

The women were startled but, as Havers had gambled, self-preservation made them step back inside. Shutting the door behind him, Havers looked at the trembling women and the gun barrel he was pointing at them.

"Apologies, but we needed to be inside. This building is being watched. Those people in the red hatchback across the road. And I have need of some answers which I might not want them to hear." Havers extended a hand. "My name is Major Havers. I work for Her Majesty and I need to see my employee, Mr Kirkgordon. I realize you are a little in shock but your co-operation is appreciated. Oh, my gun. Here, you hold it, Miss Goodritch."

Havers handed the gun to Miss Goodritch who immediately pointed it at Havers' head. "Now sir, tell me who you are." Havers laughed.

"Handing over of a loaded gun to the general public is not standard practice, Miss Goodritch. And I never break standard practice." Havers whipped the gun from her hand and pointed it at his head before pulling the trigger six times. "I am your friend, possibly your protector, so please co-operate. I'd call the police to verify this for you but I really don't want to bring the squad cars with their lights here. So please, will you take me to Mr Kirkgordon?"

The ladies were still nervous but the landlady led the way to Kirkgordon's room.

Havers knocked on the door hard and called out Kirkgordon's name. He tried three more times, then said to the landlady, "My apologies, but I need to enter," and kicked the door through at the handle. It swung open and a fusty smell hit his nose. "I think my man was out last night." Havers examined Kirkgordon's hands and noticed a red rash on the back of one of them. Opening the eyelids, he checked the eyes and then placed his head close to Kirkgordon's chest to monitor his breathing.

"Ladies, Mr Kirkgordon is not asleep. He is in fact being held in stasis. Which means someone will come for him. I don't know who – perhaps the people in the car. This puts you in great danger and so I am going to take both of you to the local police station. We are also taking Mr Kirkgordon with us, but not through the front door. You'll have to trust me on this. If you find that difficult I can load up my gun again and be more persuasive. Trust me, you are in great danger."

The ladies stared in disbelief but Havers didn't wait for questions. Instead he touched his ear and ran quickly through HQ's password routine. Breaking his conversation, he asked the landlady for the name of the street behind the guest house. After she had answered, he repeated the information before confirming "five minutes".

"Right, ladies. We are going to leave via the rear entrance. Madam, if you would lock up the house. Don't be seen at any windows. Miss Goodritch, you will need to open the doors for me."

The ladies nodded, both slightly pale with shock. Havers took Kirkgordon and threw him over his shoulder. The fugitives exited through the rear door of the property and negotiated a small wooden fence before stepping out into the street. A red transit pulled up and the driver's window rolled down. Before the driver, a young fair-haired man, could say anything, Havers spoke.

"Visionary! Yes, you heard me, Visionary. Yes, I know, you never thought you'd hear that codeword. But this is for real, so look lively, gentlemen. Now, assist these ladies into the back and then straight to your station. You stop for no one."

The driver gulped but gave an affirmative nod before jumping out and opening the rear of the van. After seeing his passengers aboard, he returned to the driver's seat and sped off. Meanwhile, the two people in the red hatchback continued to stare at the front door of the guest house. They were unaware of the local street camera now turning its attention to them. Neither were they aware that their names and addresses were being displayed on Havers' mobile phone.

His operation had been compromised. Supernatural indicators were off the scale. And one of his people was dead. Inside the cool and calm exterior, a rage was building, a hunger for revenge. Relax, Arthur, he told himself, relax. Time for a chat with Miss Goodritch.

Observations

The lab boys back at HQ had been very helpful. There was more to Kirkgordon's incapacitation than Havers had first thought. The dosage, of a compound he hadn't even heard of, was so large that Kirkgordon was going to be out until at least tomorrow. Clearly there was some motive in taking him out for so long but what, exactly? Havers couldn't make sense of it. Wilson had probably seen something. So they killed him. Well, that was the assumption. But Kirkgordon had merely been drugged and watched, suggesting a future need of some sort. But what need?

Havers had given thought to removing Austerley from the care home, but the policemen who visited on a bogus call confirmed Austerley was there and peaceful, if not conscious. Anyway, extracting Austerley would arouse suspicion, and the perpetrators would probably go underground with their secret. He needed to understand, to build a picture. He was convinced Wilson must have been on to something. Hopefully Miss Goodritch would yield some help.

Havers entered the police interview room and crossed the floor to shake hands with Jane Goodritch. Her face looked a little worn with worry but otherwise she seemed in good health, maintaining the rounded smile which matched her plump disposition.

"Sorry to have to be in here. I'd rather sit in a café somewhere and have a more pleasant chat, Miss Goodritch," said Havers.

"Jane, call me Jane. I understand this is important. The constable, when I asked him, said it wasn't that he *wouldn't* tell me who you were but that he *couldn't*. So you must be of some importance." Jane folded her arms nervously.

"My work is important, Jane, not me. I'm a servant to this country like us all, I'm afraid. And yes, what is going on at the moment is important and not for discussion outside these walls, if we understand each other."

"Certainly." Jane coughed.

Why do I always make people nervous even when I'm being nice? thought Havers. Then he remembered the gun.

"Apologies for holding a gun at you, but your life was in danger. To keep you safe I needed your co-operation, not your gratitude."

"Thank you. I think."

"Now, please tell me everything you know about Mr Kirkgordon. It's his surname, by the way."

"Right. What's his first name?"

"That's probably something he should divulge himself. Anyway, what do you know of our Mr Kirkgordon?"

Jane Goodritch spent the next half hour recounting Kirkgordon's visit to her arts centre and the history of the town. Focusing intently, Havers made notes on a small pad.

"You say they hung him up on the hill?" asked Havers.

"Yes, the viewing spot, Gibbet Point. Do you know it?" Jane replied.

"Yes, Jane. I was up there this afternoon. Now that is worrying. Are there any elements in the town who take these stories seriously?"

"Well, I take them seriously."

"Indeed, Jane, indeed you do. As do I. I was meaning, are there any groups who take these matters seriously but with more of an evil intent?"

"Evil intent?"

"Yes, Jane. Evil. Curses and the like and revenge of this sort don't just happen. Usually, some influence from the earthly world is required to readmit the spirit world. I was wondering if there were any particular people who might be so disposed to try this."

"To be honest, Major Havers, I don't know of anything occult or evil, witchcraft or anything like that. We're just a quiet little town with a bit of history."

"Much obliged," said Havers. "I need to get Mr Kirkgordon to someone who can watch over him properly and, as you have been seen in contact with him, I would suggest you accompany me and place yourself under the protection of a colleague. Just for a day or so, until we clear this all up. It's probably nothing, but best to be safe."

"Do you really think I'm in danger?"

If the indicators are right we're all in for it, thought Havers. "Probably nothing," he said. "Don't worry too much about it. Just a precaution."

Time was starting to press and Havers decided that the care home would be his main reconnaissance. But first he would need to organize back-up in case the situation was as he feared. A swift call to HQ put the wheels in motion before Havers exited the police station in an unmarked car with Miss Goodritch up front and a prone Kirkgordon lying across the back seat.

The evening was drawing in as the car pulled into the church car park. Before Havers could open the car door, the priest was already reaching for the handle. He had a worried look on his face.

"You're here without a disguise. Is it that bad?" asked Father Jonah.

"It may be. Indeed, it may be. But it is good to see an old friend," replied Havers.

"Old friend?" The priest laughed. "You must want something, Arthur. The f-word never appears unless you want something. But I am magnanimous. God bless you anyway."

"I do need help. Mr Kirkgordon is in the back of the car and is under the influence of some nasty sedatives. His cure has been administered, but the reaction time means he won't see anything of this day. Somebody did this to him and I need him protected. The lady in the car—"

"Jane Goodritch."

"Ah, good, you know her. Well, she's tangled up in it now too. So just to be safe, keep an eye on her, please."

"Strangers in distress. I believe I am commanded to help by our dear Lord. By the way, good choice in Mr Kirkgordon."

"Why do you say that?"

"Well, he never believes a word you say. Smart man."

"Unfair," countered Havers. "Well, I have a bit of watching to do tonight but I'll drop by for breakfast."

"Of course, you'll be most welcome. My daughter does some excellent mussels."

"Still at that old trick?" Havers chuckled. "Well, Father Jonah, be ready! We may require sanctuary."

The priest nodded before collecting Miss Goodritch and then carrying Kirkgordon inside with Havers' help.

Night had fallen by the time Havers had changed into his

camouflage outfit. Urban colour and pattern for this job, he had reckoned, and so he wore a mix of blacks and greys. Over the years, he had grown a great disdain for the paint he had to put on his face as his skin reacted ever so slightly to it. More a nuisance than anything else but still annoying. Not that he ever allowed this gem of information to be passed on.

With the car parked some five hundred metres away, Havers moved silently through the streets and reached a vantage point in the shrubs where the only road in and out of the care home passed by. He settled down for a long wait, listening to the sound of the sea in the distance. It reminded him of his feelings at Gibbet Point so he tried to take his mind elsewhere.

They had said he wasn't cut out for a life of service in the secret divisions of the military. MI5 had rejected him out of hand. He had pushed himself hard through various training courses, learned how to fight in many different styles and achieved fluency in three languages, but his background was always seen as too risky. It had hardly been his fault that his father had delved into the black arts. Dad, he thought, you always pushed the limits, always wanted that which was out of reach.

The event which would be his father's downfall turned out to be the making of Havers. It's not every man in his twenties who takes on a summoned demon and wins. Win: it's such a short, sweeping word. Yes, I vanquished it. Yes, I sealed it away for good. And yes, I saved a lot of lives that day. But I lost you, Dad. I lost you. There was no choice, no chance to get you back after you had summoned it. And I did it like you taught me – always focused, weighing the needs, getting the job done. I always get the job done.

There were various comings and goings at the care home

with many people visiting their relatives or friends on a Sunday night before the busy week ahead. Havers, methodical as always, watched each of them, intently looking for anything out of place. Soon it was time for the home to be locked up. Havers saw Graham the manager waving goodnight to his staff and leaving the place in the care of his night crew.

And there was that girl again, the one who had come into Austerley's room. He noticed she was watching carefully as Graham left and stood at the door observing for another ten minutes after he had gone. Doors were locked and lights all turned down low.

The next three hours were dull. Absolutely nothing happened. Or, to be exact, as Havers always was, nothing apart from the fox which he saw lurking in the car park for five minutes before it caught a scent and scampered off. And the hedgehog which ambled its way right past him.

At about 2 am he saw movement in the home and then a figure exiting the front door. They were dressed in black and began to search the immediate vicinity of the care home. The figure moved in a simple pattern and Havers was able to avoid them easily as they approached. Evidently satisfied with their search, the person returned to the home and could be seen through the glass with a telephone in hand.

Two minutes later a black van arrived. Four figures exited the care home briefly and opened up the doors, including a large sliding one on the side of the van. Havers watched them return to the building and then re-emerge carrying two bodies, one of which Havers recognized immediately. Austerley. And there's his missing foot to confirm it.

Having dumped their cargo into the van, all four figures climbed on board and the van drove off serenely. Havers noted the plate as it went by and with a flick of his wrist threw a small tracker, no bigger than a slice of carrot, onto the side of the van. He waited for a few minutes to make sure the action had moved on before returning to his car.

On sitting down at the driver's seat he switched on the computer interface and selected his tracker software. Good, he thought, it's working. The tracker software showed the van entering the lower car park for the town's viewpoint, Gibbet Point. Havers drove to a spot some distance from the car park and followed the alternative path to the hill top. Mentally checking his armoury, Havers hoped there would be no encounters. This was strictly reconnaissance.

At the top he was able to find a dark spot in the bracken. Crouching down, he saw six figures approach Gibbet Point via the main path. Two of the figures appeared to be walking in a drunken state. One had to be supported because he was missing a foot. Austerley. The figure at the front was slight, but attractive.

Austerley and the other man were dumped unceremoniously on the ground while the slight figure began to remove her outer clothing. It's that nurse, thought Havers. The one from Austerley's room. The other three figures crowded over Austerley's companion and began to chant. Havers watched as the chanting increased. The nurse cried out in a bizarre language unknown to Havers and shed her remaining clothes. Any erotic thoughts were driven from Havers' mind by the sound of the language. It wasn't just guttural but positively hellish.

The man on the floor cried out and Havers could see, by what poor light there was, the man's features start to shrink. Before Havers' eyes, the man's hair began to fall out and his nose and ears grew significantly. Blotches appeared on the skin and, without warning, the man's joints began to contract. He was shrivelling up.

Time to intervene, thought Havers, and he reached inside his outfit to press a button. At HQ, the loudest alarm rang and agents who had previously been spending a quiet night shift sprang to life. Drawing a gun from within his garb, Havers checked it was loaded and pushed through the bracken.

Before him, an apparition began to form, intensely luminous with a distinct tri-cornered hat. After firing off three shots directly into the rapidly forming pirate, Havers fell back as a neon cutlass blade sliced the air.

"Say your prayers, soldier, Captain Smith's back!"

Gibbet Point

avers rolled backwards, clear of the first swipe of the cutlass. With one hand he reached deep into his clothing and activated the panic button to alert HQ. The other hand was still on his gun, firing at the apparition before him. It was dressed like a swashbuckler from the movies, complete with buttoned longcoat and pantaloons, but the face was one of decay, with pieces of green flesh attached sporadically to a luminous skull. The eyes were missing from the sockets and there was just a hole for its nose.

After Havers' initial panic had passed, he realized the bullets were passing straight through the ghost. Pocketing his gun, he reached inside his clothing and retrieved two wooden sticks with short stumpy handles on each end. Taking one handle in each hand and allowing the sticks to run the length of his forearms, Havers stood his ground against the ghastly Captain Smith.

"You'll feel my blade, son," hissed the ghost as it lunged forward with an almighty swipe of its cutlass. Havers parried the blade with one of his sticks and drove his other forearm into Captain Smith's skull. The ghost was thrown backwards and its spectral hat fell from its head.

"You're not the first thing from hell that I've seen. And I sent the rest back to their pit." Havers was not a particularly large man but now he was looming over the ghost.

"But I rarely venture alone," said Smith. "Lads, get this ship rat!"

Greenish figures appeared from thin air. Deckhands swinging knives and clubs were running towards Havers. The longer grass parted as the pirates rushed past. Havers' mind seized this detail and built a plan on it. Looking around desperately, Havers spotted an old archway, filled up with concrete but with an alcove of some six feet. Well, he thought, there's nothing else for it. Havers ran to the doorway and turned to face his foes. It was a horde. There must have been nearly sixty of them. This is it, Arthur, he told himself. No surrender, no retreat. There's no mercy and no escape. Focus and let loose. Send this filth back to hell!

Havers pulled two more short pieces of wood from his clothing and dropped them into neat slits on the shins of his trouser legs. The first pirate was on him, thrusting a knife. Havers stepped to one side and launched an almighty kick to its midriff, causing a cracking sound which split the air. Havers marvelled at how even ghostly ribs can be cracked when hit with the right tools. The apparition dropped to the ground, felling two others behind it. Havers brought both arms straight down onto their heads, cracking both skulls.

Sometimes it would be handy if ghostly bodies would behave in the same way as human ones, thought Havers. A body pile in front of him would have been a good shield for this fight. But the bodies just faded away, their glow disappearing. The initial blows struck by Havers had caused reluctance amongst the pirate horde to be at the front of the attack. Havers laughed, remembering his younger days and his first fight. No one likes to disappoint those in charge. They may have come from hell but they wanted to stay on earth, not return as vanquished souls and have to explain their failure to an unsympathetic boss.

"Take him now, lads, and be quick about it! Or I'll hang every one of you from the yardarm and feed you to the hounds of hell." The rally from Captain Smith caused a panic, but as the captain slew one of the deckhands at the rear of the charge, the horde raced forward again.

Havers was cool and methodical as he smashed and bludgeoned his way through the horde. Taking the odd blow from a fist or a foot, he avoided all weapons as he tore through the ranks. The protection of the alcove meant he faced a front of only three to four attackers at a time. Gambling that the rules controlling their manifestation in this realm meant they could not pass through solid concrete, Havers didn't even glance behind him, taking his untouched back as the only assurance he needed. But there was no easy escape and he doubted any help would be found within the hour.

Gradually the ranks of the deckhands thinned and Havers thought he saw his opportunity for escape. Stepping inside the lunge of a sword, he smashed his right arm into one of the figures before racing forward in berserker fashion. Like a whirling dervish, he spun and struck and struck again. With a ten second burst, he broke the ranks on his left-hand side and sprinted for his life. There was a two hundred metre run until the bracken and bushes which would impede both himself and his pursuers, but he was banking on being the more nimble.

The blood pumped hard around his body and he forced himself to breathe in a controlled and measured way, focusing on the first bracken to be struck aside. Not once did he turn to look at the scene behind him, as he knew that any slowing of the pace would have the horde on him without protection on any flank. Ten metres to go and Havers was swinging his arm to clear the bracken when he heard the wind whoosh above him. What was that? To look would be folly so he merely swished the air above him and dived into the bracken.

As his feet left the ground in the dive, he felt talons rip into his shoulders. The claws sunk in beside his rotator cuffs and he was carried up into the air. Whatever creature it was went into an almost vertical climb before turning back towards where Havers had run from. Captain Smith was laughing. The creature swooped and dropped Havers from six feet up, causing him to clatter hard into the ground. Despite this, Havers turned his messy fall into a forward roll and was just rising up from the ground when he was caught on the chest by a large boot. It pinned him to the floor and a cutlass with a pointed tip was placed in the middle of his face.

"And we'll take the life from this one too," laughed the captain.

Breathless and bruised, Havers lay back knowing that for the moment he was trapped. But his mind was still working hard, looking for even the smallest advantage and the opportunity for escape that it might bring.

Beside him, a winged beast landed and lunged forward with its long neck. The beast had a black eagle's head and talons, and its leathery deep-blue wings were complemented by two massive human arms which ended in claws. With twitching movements, the beast kept one eye on the prone Havers. Smith stepped forward and ripped the wooden weapons from the government man.

"The wood is from this realm so how did these strike me?"

Captain Smith asked his captive.

Havers spat some blood from his mouth onto the ground. "Magic!" he answered and stared up at the unholy pirate.

"It does not matter. Nothing matters now. Not now my love has brought me back. Now is the time to rule this place. Captive, have you ever been to hell?"

"Hell, *c'est les autres*! Especially you!"

"Come. You will see power. You will see men broken by my will. You will see a lord in this place. They rebuked me and now they will suffer. Revenge will be visited on their generations. They will burn." The captain turned to the other captives. Austerley was looking extremely dopey, probably from the drugs. The other captive had been forced to the ground on his knees. The four people who had brought him now gathered around him and placed their hands on him. And then the chanting began.

It was off-key, off-tone, off-pitch. Everything that gives music its natural beauty had been stripped away and replaced by a distortion of alarming proportions. Havers grabbed his ears to block out the sounds and Austerley became more agitated. The man on his knees rocked and reeled under their touch.

Havers became strangely engrossed as he looked at the man. Horrified but mystified, he watched as lines began to form across the man's face. His nose grew along with his ears, hair sprouting from both. The body buckled and started to wither inward, with his chest collapsing, his legs thinning and his hair falling out in large clumps. Beside him danced the nurse from the care home, offering up her flesh to the night. Havers saw her face change as she danced. It took on a horrid grin and her eyes became wild.

The withering man collapsed to the ground. His shrunken

body was significantly smaller than when they had begun.

The captain kicked the body over and called on his deckhands to remove the jetsam. He moved towards the nurse and roared into the night, "Now we shall take this place away, to the depths of hell, to rule side by side, my dear. And when I have fed on this one's life, I shall find and take that body you want for me."

Austerley was dragged forward and thrown to his knees. Havers caught a glimpse of Austerley's face and saw the look of horror on it. Even in his dreams of Dagon, Austerley had never looked so terrified. But Havers also realized that Austerley was becoming fully awake in his terror. Focus, Arthur, focus, the moment's coming, he thought.

The chanting began again but this time in a different language, and the nurse did not place her hands on the victim but broke off to be at Captain Smith's side.

"Dance, my dear, dance! Celebrate our victory," howled Smith into the night. The nurse began to spin around in unholy erotic poses, much to the captain's delight. Fighting to keep his attention away from her mesmeric movements, Havers fixed his eyes on Austerley, who began to undergo the change. His thick, wild hair started to drop out in clumps. The jowls on his face tightened and his back hunched tighter. From an obese start, Austerley was shedding so much weight he was starting to look like a starving refugee. But then there was a new noise. Austerley was also beginning to chant.

Meanwhile, the black night was changing. In the sky a fireball erupted and began to grow. A fierce heat radiated from it and it seemed to streak across the horizon, encircling the town. The captain laughed as it grew, occasionally grabbing his mistress with erotic intent, happy for her to be on show. Austerley looked wretched, a poor parody of the man he had been, but, with an inner resolve, he began to stand up. His chanting was now a raging cacophony, enough to grab the captain's attention.

Havers had no idea what Austerley was doing but the chanting was engrossing everyone, including the winged beast that stood guard over him. Spotting an opportunity, he moved ever so subtly towards his fighting sticks, which were lying just beside the beast.

The ground began to shake and the whole vista caught fire. Captain Smith laughed pointedly at Austerley, who was still chanting even with three people trying to push him back down. Then the earth fell away.

It was like being on a fairground ride with the earth as the car. Everything seemed to drop vertically. The captain and his horde yelled with delight and he grabbed his lover by the waist, celebrating with a brutal kiss. Havers felt sick but concentrated on reaching his sticks. From the corner of his eye he saw Austerley straighten up and his three oppressors fall to the ground. Then the falling sensation stopped like a lift coming to an abrupt halt. All those standing, except for Austerley, tumbled to the ground.

Havers had been lying down so was unaffected by the abrupt halt. He grabbed his sticks and leapt up at the winged beast, which had collapsed flat on the ground, its feet having given way under it. With speed, precision and above all, power, Havers buried a stick into the beast's head. Without waiting to see if his action had been successful, Havers ran to Austerley and swept him onto his shoulder in an impromptu fireman's lift. By the time Smith and his horde had reacted, Havers was already racing down the hillside with his prize.

Austerley was babbling. The same statements repeated over and over, as if he were convincing himself all was not lost.

"Churchy, they need Churchy. Manifesting, full flesh. Stupid idiot, she wanted him. Consummation, flesh. Need Churchy. Halted now. Halted now but not complete. Not safe, not safe. Havers, find Churchy. Find Churchy."

Escape

Bracken ripped at his trousers as he crashed through. With Austerley over his shoulder, Havers couldn't bend down far enough to swipe the deeper tangles clear of his legs but had to plough through regardless. The roar behind him spurred him on and he was able to see quite well due to the light from the fire in the sky. The world was like a well-lit dining hall of old and, while not the same as daylight, it did illuminate all but the darkest corners.

There were three vehicles in the car park at the bottom of Gibbet Point. Two looked modern, and Havers knew that breaking through their defences would take longer than he had. The other car he remembered as being brought out some ten years ago and it looked to be the basic model. This was a good time to start his life as a carjacker.

Austerley was unceremoniously dumped on the car bonnet and Havers drove his elbow through the driver's window. It was crass but time didn't allow for finesse. He then drove the handles of his sticks into the radiator grill, leaving the length of the sticks parallel to the front of the car, like bull bars. He opened the door, pushed Austerley into the passenger seat and followed inside, grabbing his colleague's legs and whipping them out of the way. Havers then reached underneath the steering wheel and ripped open the interior. He was dimly aware of the pirate horde charging down the hill but maintained his cool, calm, dispassionate self as he worked on the wiring.

The engine fired into life and Havers spun the wheel, driving the car across a grassy area and striking down several deck-hands in the process. As the wheels fought for grip on the grass, Havers remembered his driving lessons and coaxed the car onto the path. He avoided the main route out to the road as this would take him alongside the descending horde. He believed they might just be able to hold on to a car so he took the walker's path instead. Havers switched on the car lights and a tree appeared in his vision. He flung the car hard left, causing Austerley to roll sideways and strike his head on the passenger door.

Without looking behind him, Havers concentrated on the track ahead. It was extremely narrow and he clipped shrubs and bushes in rapid succession. Turning a corner on the path, Havers was confronted by a small bridge. Its width looked similar to that of the car but Havers was not stopping. The sides of the bridge buckled as the wing mirrors were ripped off. The hubcaps were squeezed off and Havers heard a tyre burst. The car bounced clear on the other side of the bridge and began to pull to one side. Fighting against it, Havers tried to recall his intended route.

"Where the hell are you going?" yelled Austerley.

"Sanctuary. You're off to church, Mr Austerley. It's about time you paid a visit."

"Watch out for the cops!" Austerley's warning, while timely, was unnecessary. Spinning the wheel, Havers slid his vehicle past the white car with the flashing blue lights. In his rear-view mirror, he saw the horde descend on the emergency vehicle and flip it into the air. Austerley screamed out but Havers remained calm and focused. Racing down a narrow street he could see a spire in the distance. Thank you, God, he thought, for instilling in your believers a desire for prominence.

Austerley was babbling. "Churchy, they need Churchy. She wants him, needs him. Wants to have him. So they can have relations. Difficult between spirit and flesh. Too difficult. Need Churchy."

Havers tried to ignore Austerley's words but something inside was already analysing these ideas. The other terror that raged within Havers was the thought that there were possibly eight thousand people in their beds who were prey for this pirate horde. And I can't protect them, thought Havers. I have nothing for them.

One doorway caught Havers' attention as he sped past it. In the blur of the moment, it seemed that there was a burning cross on the door. It made no sense to Havers and he shouted at Austerley to look.

"I see it! Cross on fire, Havers. I see it. No idea what it is but I see it," said Austerley.

Havers swung the car hard into a car park and Austerley could see that they had arrived at a building with a large spire. There was a priest standing in the car park. The priest walked past the car to the edge of the building's grounds. The pirate horde then rounded the corner but stopped abruptly at the car park's edge. Captain Smith pushed his deckhands to the side as he strode to the front, eyes fixed on the priest. In Smith's wake came the nurse, Tania, naked and walking with a swagger.

"Enjoying this, priest?" provoked Tania, parading herself with no dignity.

"Be gone, witch, you have no charms to interest me," replied the priest, his eyes never flinching from Captain Smith.

"We want the one you call Kirkgordon," said Captain Smith. "Give him to me or I'll rip your throat out. I'll spike your soul with hellfire and—"

"Silence, beast!" The priest's words thundered out. "This is sanctuary and your words shall not be permitted."

Havers had exited the car and now stood with the priest. He watched as Smith turned to his rabble and waved his cutlass in the air. The deckhands opened their mouths to yell but Havers heard nothing. It was like someone had turned off the sound at a rock concert. Arms waved, fists shook, but all was quiet.

Smith signalled a charge and the deckhands raced forward. Havers turned to run but the priest stood motionless. The first deckhand to step onto the car park turned from a ghostly form into a mere trace of luminous smoke. Those behind him combusted in a similar fashion. Quickly the surge stopped and the horde quietened, wondering what had happened.

"This is sanctuary!" bawled the priest, "and the citizens of hell are not welcome." He turned his back on the horde and smiled at an astounded Havers. "Well, Arthur, I don't know about you, but I could murder a cuppa. Should we give your friend a hand?"

"Okay, Ohlos, I haven't seen anything quite like that before. A little protective ring around a person or a small group, yes, but actually covering a whole building? Lethal to them as well. Very impressive, my friend." Havers sipped his tea, letting his statement hang, begging a response.

"It isn't just the church, Arthur. There's more than that." The statement from the priest wasn't proud, just matter-of-fact.

"Ah, yes, the burning cross on the doors. Incredible. All the people of the town trapped in and the evil trapped out. I am impressed, Ohlos. Truly impressed, for once."

"I was doubtful I could do it but with our descent interrupted the influence is much stronger."

"Ohlos, although impressed, I am also confused. Our descent? Do you mean to hell?" Havers raised his eyebrows.

"I find it hard to believe you've never been. But yes, you are correct. Descent is a figurative word here. We have not moved into the ground here but across, how shall I put this, other planes? The motion we felt was from that movement, but someone stopped it. Someone prevented us from reaching the other side. And so we see the fire in the sky."

"Hellfire?"

"No, Arthur. It's just a physical manifestation of the boundary. We are in limbo. A place between. And that is as far as my understanding goes. We are in another place. Exactly where... well, I don't know." The priest dropped his chin, staring at his tea.

"What's wrong, Ohlos?" asked Havers.

"We won't stay here. At least, I doubt it. Something will give and when it does we will descend, and all this protection will go. We need a reversal, some way to put it back. But I don't know how."

"I have a man that might. I think it is time we assemble all our players. Find out what's required. Time for you to meet Mr Austerley. I warn you, he's not too keen on clergy."

"With all the troubles in the news, no one is. I'm pretty used to it."

Havers disappeared through the living room door and then reappeared with Austerley hobbling behind him. Holding the door handle to steady himself, Austerley looked the priest up and down, noting with disgust the clerical collar.

"Mr Austerley, please meet Father Jonah," announced Havers.

"Are you here to sink us?" snapped Austerley.

"It's towards the back of that book, isn't it? I never read it, at least not that section. But to control it! There's one alive in you, isn't there? Dreams, dreams that cripple. Excuse the pun." Father Jonah looked into Austerley's eyes. "May God have mercy on you. You saw Dagon."

"Face to face, priest," spat Austerley.

"And it was only the efforts of Mr Kirkgordon and myself that rescued him from it," said Havers.

"He shot my foot! I have no foot because of that arse. You and Churchy can stick your rescue mission," raged Austerley.

"Churchy?" asked the priest.

"Mr Kirkgordon," Havers enlightened him. "They have pet names for each other. Dear friends, really."

"And you stopped the descent! Mr Austerley, I am impressed. Please, take a seat."

The compliment made Austerley beam and he became less cantankerous. Havers stood and helped the prematurely aged occult professor to a seat. A moment later, Kirkgordon entered the room. Austerley glared at him.

"What happened to you? I said you shouldn't smoke. Bloody bad for you," said Kirkgordon.

"You can piss off, Churchy. Some bloody protector, you!" Austerley's wizened face became even more contorted in anger.

"I was drugged. Our friend the priest has worked wonders in getting me back on my feet. Anyway, you were in a care home and you couldn't even look after yourself in there."

"Gentlemen, enough," ordered Havers. "When we get

everything sorted I will happily let you kick the verbal knackers off each other but until then you are on my payroll and will behave. Understand me? Good. Ohlos, bring my colleagues up to speed, please."

Father Jonah outlined what he knew and Austerley became quite pained. Once the priest had finished, Austerley leaned forward in his chair to speak and the others remained silent.

"The padre is right about where we are. And he's right we won't stay here. It's complicated, but the barriers I put in place with my chants won't hold forever. There's a spirit returned to wreak havoc on this town for some reason. An old pirate, I think. Privateer, to be accurate. He is the threat, and when commanding his crew he is dangerous, but he's not in flesh form yet. He needs to take on a physical form. He's to inhabit a live body. And that body is you, Churchy."

"Me! Why the hell me?"

"Because she likes you. That nurse you were flirting with in the home. The one whose arse you kept checking out. The one you took out for a drink. She's a witch, draining life from people and giving it to her beloved."

"Bloody hell," gasped Kirkgordon.

"And she wants your body. That dance she was doing signified lust and hunger."

"How does a little dancing make her a witch? Just because she got a bit jiggy with it."

"Churchy, she was naked, exposing herself like a top shelf magazine. It's occult dancing. It's very intoxicating and it calls up things from hell."

"She's probably being used."

"No, Churchy, she's the core, she's the one who started this, and now she's riding like a hooker on the arm of a spirit. And a right bastard of a one at that."

"Damn, I was an alarm call from bedding her." The room fell silent as they stared at him.

"I guess the time with your wife did not go so well, then?" proposed Havers.

"It's complicated," rallied Kirkgordon, but he hung his head in shame. "It's bloody complicated." I know my sins will find me out, thought Kirkgordon, but a witch? That's just unfair, damn well unfair.

Plans

There were six of them assembled in the living room. A government agent, a former protector, a historical building curator, an expert on the occult and all things fantastical and a priest with his twelve-year-old daughter. Outside, outwith the grounds of the church whose manse they were sitting in, was a horde from hell, devilish ghostly pirates led by a captain with his naked lover in tow, a lover who had been a nurse at the town's care home before summoning the captain and draining life from the home's residents. It isn't the craziest situation I've found myself in, thought Havers, but it's close.

"We need to pool our knowledge and thinking on this matter, everyone, as I don't believe any of us have a full picture on what is happening yet." Havers scanned the assembly, seeking any discontent. "Let's start with our expert. Mr Austerley, tell us what you know."

"I know I'm a lot older than I should be! You could've intervened a bit quicker, Havers." Austerley shook his head at his treatment so far.

"One, Mr Austerley, that doesn't help. Two, you find me anyone else who could have extracted you from such a horde armed only with some wooden sticks and I will hire them immediately and head for the Costa del Sol and a happier life. And three, kindly answer the question and show these good people why I felt it necessary to save your precious skin in the first place." Havers held his stare.

Austerley looked annoyed. "Well, if that's the—"

"Four, I refer you to point three. Now, what do you know?"

Austerley glowered at Havers but focused on the task at hand. "Not a lot, if truth be told. When I was in the care home, one of the nurses, specifically Kirkgordon's naked chick—"

"Hey, that's unfair!" interjected Kirkgordon.

"Enough, Mr Austerley. The details please," insisted Havers.

"Well, she wore a rather peculiar necklace with a swirling symbol that looked familiar. So I asked Havers to get a certain book from a Swiss library so that I could learn more about it. I was drugged before I could read the book, and I woke up on Gibbet Point having the life drained from me before Havers kindly took matters into his own hands." Austerley nodded his appreciation at Havers.

"Continue," said Havers.

"Well, I have now been able to study the book and can say that earlier assertions are correct. She is a witch, and a dangerous one. But also a possessed one."

"Possessed?" asked Kirkgordon, "How?"

"Generally by a spirit coming into the body and setting up house. What sort of detail are you looking for?"

"There's no need to be like that, Indy."

"Who's Indy?" asked the priest's daughter.

"Sorry, just a name for Austerley. Because he's so Indiana Jones. Can't keep his nose out of any artefact," responded Kirkgordon.

Havers took charge of the conversation again. "Enough,

everyone, let Mr Austerley continue."

"It's the design, you see. It's very old and comes from a line of witches who passed down their knowledge through the generations. I suspect that Captain Smith's bitch—" Austerley saw Havers' eyes flash fire and his face indicate with a nod that there were ladies present. "Sorry, his lady, was probably part of the line, as is the nurse."

"She's only eighteen, Austerley. How do you get into a line of witches at eighteen?" demanded Kirkgordon. "There didn't seem to be much of a witch about her at all."

"On the contrary, Mr Kirkgordon," said a passive Havers, "she almost seduced a married man who should have been alert to outside influences. She also appeared in Austerley's room just as I was about to discover evidence. Oh, and she danced an erotic, blasphemous dance and stared right at me with eyes shining with hellfire. And I know hellfire! So, for an eighteen-year-old, she showed a number of signs."

Kirkgordon folded his arms like a spoilt child. I didn't even sleep with her, he thought.

"Now, if we can continue," said Havers. "After all, it's only the lives and souls of this town that are on the line. Mr Austerley?"

"My difficulty is in pinpointing the branch of witch lore she comes from. There are fourteen possible options, although three of those are so little used that I find it unlikely they would be employed here. The necklace symbol, although rare, is too vague. It shows witchery in general but not the specific type. Was there anything else she touched or was concerned about?"

"I don't know if it means anything but there was a brooch," offered Kirkgordon. "It was on the bedside of a patient. One of the older ladies was complaining about it but Tania shifted her on smartly."

"A brooch?" asked Havers. "What sort?"

"Emerald, I think, with diamonds and some writing."

"That was beside Mr Austerley's bed too. It was there when she hurried me out of his room," said Havers.

"Get it for me. I need to see it," demanded Austerley.

"Okay," said Havers, "time for a little walk, Mr Kirkgordon. Maybe Nefol, too."

"Who?" asked Kirkgordon.

Havers pointed at the twelve-year-old girl.

Shaking his head, Kirkgordon railed, "Why the hell would you risk a child's protection by taking her out there?"

"Mr Kirkgordon, it's no risk. She's going for your protection." Kirkgordon looked at the priest in desperation but all he got in return was a smiling nod. Sitting back into his seat, Kirkgordon despaired at the madness his work involved him in these days.

"Search the building," said Austerley, "and bring anything else interesting you find."

"It's not like we have loads of time, Indy," complained Kirkgordon. "If you hadn't noticed, the place is crawling with ghosts and I'm just guessing this sanctuary doesn't cover the care home. And as it stands, apart from Havers' sticks, we are low on weapons."

"Mr Austerley is right though, Mr Kirkgordon. We need to search the place. And as for weapons, I suspect our priest has something lurking in his cupboards." Havers was clearly agitated by Kirkgordon's continued interruptions. "The other matter we need to address is our lack of knowledge about the history of these episodes. Miss Goodritch, I believe you can be of some help in consultation with Mr Austerley, but he would like to go further than a mere verbal exchange."

"Miss Goodritch," began Austerley.

"Jane, please, just Jane."

"Ah, Jane. Havers said you were the local expert on the town's history. I'll need to tap into that expertise in order to understand where this Captain Smith is coming from. But, more than that, I'll need to see and touch any artefacts you have."

"Really," said Jane, fascinated.

"Oh, yes. When one has a disposition such as mine, the mere presence of a device or memorial of power will alert my occult senses. I am what they call attuned. It's why they fear me."

Kirkgordon burst out laughing.

"Mr Kirkgordon, this is not the time," snapped an angry Havers. "Kindly contain your juvenile one-upmanship with Mr Austerley. There is work to be done."

"So who's going to get these artefacts, Havers?" countered Kirkgordon. "Again, there's a load of ghosts running around the neighbourhood and Austerley's one foot short of a sprint."

"Just concentrate on your job and leave that to the experts, Mr Kirkgordon. Your candour is becoming quite annoying."

"One important point," announced the priest, standing. "If you get into difficulty you can run into any sanctuary I have set up. All the houses, garages, coffee shops, whatever. However, you will then be trapped. I couldn't risk the general public leaving their abodes once I had set up the refuges. Only I can let you out. And I need to be with you to do it. Are we understood?" There was a murmur of agreement. "Good. Now, a moment of prayer."

Kirkgordon watched Austerley roll his eyes when the priest bowed his head. Finding it hard to focus, Kirkgordon made the motion of closing his eyes, but in his head he was addressing God directly: You couldn't have pointed out she was a witch? I mean it's not like I'd have just ended up having an affair. I would have been her demonic lover if it had all gone to plan. Great job of looking out for me.

Then another voice entered his head: Sanctuary. You seem to be in the right place despite your stupid actions. I guess someone else was doing my job!

When the prayer was finished, Kirkgordon stood up and approached Havers. Havers' eyes warned that the next question had better be sensible.

"Havers, are you sure you're covered? I mean, taking Austerley with his foot and the woman as well. She's no athlete."

"If I needed help, I would have asked. Understand this, Mr Kirkgordon. When this place was getting dragged, flown, dropped or whatever the verb is for it, the only one who stopped it was Mr Austerley. He is an extremely potent weapon, like so many of the people in this room. You need to stop bemoaning their faults and start building them up and using them. They are all terrified underneath, and with good cause. So I need you to start being a leader and a source of unity or I will drop you. And I use drop in our professional sense. Am I clear?"

Damn it, Havers, you're as clear as you are cold, thought Kirkgordon. Ice to the core. Consummate professional. I hope Her Majesty is proud of her employee. Despite the inner turmoil, Kirkgordon just nodded.

The priest led Kirkgordon out of the room and took him to another door in the corridor. It led to a flight of stairs which descended into the depths of the manse. At the bottom of the descent, Father Jonah flicked a light switch. Kirkgordon gasped at the sight.

The room was dimly lit but Kirkgordon could see that it housed four rows of racks, each just over a man tall. On the racks were weapons of all shapes and sizes. Each row was at least twenty feet long. It looked like no manse basement he knew. Slipping past him from behind came Nefol. Kirkgordon noticed how nimble and balanced she was. Walking to the end of the first row, she jumped onto the top rack and lifted a small shield and what looked like a dainty swinging mace.

"Doesn't she want something more substantial?" asked Kirkgordon.

"Well," said the priest, "she is only young and cannot lift the heavier items effectively. But she has balance and guile. As Havers said, she is there for your protection. Do not worry about my daughter."

Kirkgordon nodded. Things were never how they seemed in this game.

"Oh, and Mr Kirkgordon," added the priest, "He is there and He saw you to here."

"Who?" asked Kirkgordon.

"The one you blame for all this. Don't worry, He can take the anger. But remember, you cannot!"

For a moment, Kirkgordon started to respond, but the truth of the statement prevented any crevice from being prised open. Arse, thought Kirkgordon, even halfway to hell He's got an eye on me.

"One would think that comforting," said the priest. Then Father Jonah shook his head slightly, as if coming out of a trance, and looked quizzically at Kirkgordon. "Did that make sense? Made absolutely no sense to me."

Should Have Read the Manual

Been a while since I ran through the sewers, Nefol. It never gets any more pleasant." Kirkgordon pushed the manhole cover to one side. They were blasted heavy and there was no way the girl could have lifted it. Maybe I'm just the muscle, Kirkgordon pondered, before dismissing the thought with a shake of the head.

Nefol sprang out of the sewer and ran swiftly to the corner of a house. Looking back, she waved Kirkgordon on. It seemed bizarre to him having a little green dwarf running point for him. She was dressed in an olive-coloured khaki jacket and wrap leggings with her pigtails hidden under a loose hood. Her soft tight green sports slippers made no noise as she stepped. In a child's way she looked cute, except for the mace.

Kirkgordon quickly replaced the manhole then joined Nefol at the edge of the house. The sky continued to burn, and beyond the shadows everything was clear as a sunny day but the darkness provided a solid cloak which the pair used as cover.

The house across the street had the image of a cross burning on its door. At the window, oblivious to their presence, stood a man with eyes red from crying and a worn face. He was looking up and down the street anxiously, causing Kirkgordon to believe he had someone left outside and didn't know whether they were safe. How could one know? The mobile signal didn't work here. Televisions, radios, all gone. In that house, all would be quiet on the information highway, and wasn't that really a hell in itself? Sanctuary wasn't always comfortable. Especially when it was imposed.

Nefol tapped Kirkgordon's hand and pointed ahead. Two ghostly deckhands were standing guard on the main road. Each carried a short sword and they were slumped up against lamp posts on either side of the street.

"We'll scout round them," said Nefol. "No need to engage them at the moment." Kirkgordon nodded. There was still some distance to be covered before the care home, and the quieter the journey, the better.

Before he could move, a car engine roared into life. A black saloon reversed from a driveway three houses away and sped towards the two guards, who had sprung back into a more defensive pose. One took a horn from his side and blew, but Kirkgordon heard no note despite the immense level of exertion. The car raced past the two guards and a young man showed two fingers to them.

In the wind was a noise, like a stuttering helicopter but sounding much more powerful. Kirkgordon cocked his head to try to hear more clearly. Judging by Nefol's reaction, she could hear the sound too, for she began to tense up slightly. And then a streak of black flew before their eyes. It was a winged beast with the body of a snake. Enormous fangs protruded from its mouth and a flicking tongue shot back and forth. Almost immediately the image disappeared as the beast flew after the departing car. Some fifteen seconds later the car was thrown onto the street from a height and the winged snake dived to the ground. Both guards had run to the car. It had rolled badly, smashing the windows and crumpling the roof. Inside, the young man was not moving.

One of the guards reached inside and pulled the man out of the car. He slapped his face, drawing the man back to consciousness. Kirkgordon's first instinct was to rush into battle, but he thought about the way Havers was always calm and collected, never jeopardizing any mission for the sake of an individual. Nefol was looking hard at Kirkgordon and he bowed his head slightly in regret. Shaking her head in disbelief, Nefol turned and ran towards the guard.

Oh crap, thought Kirkgordon.

Nefol was already swinging her small mace when she reached the guard, whom she caught with a blow right to the forehead. As its ghostly green presence dissipated, the man it was supporting fell to the ground. Nefol ignored him as the winged snake started to attack her with quick, lunging strikes, its teeth exposed. Nefol was nimble on her feet and moved with the grace of a professional acrobat. Her mace struck the beast several times but seemed to be having little effect.

From behind Nefol, the other guard approached with his sword pointed at Nefol's back. Kirkgordon saw the danger and fired off one of Father Jonah's arrows. The shot was true, but just as he fired, Nefol swung the mace behind her and it caught the ghost on the top of its head, knocking it sideways while Kirkgordon's arrow flew past harmlessly. However, the guard paid for that good fortune as Nefol swung the mace again and finished off the ghost with a blow to the side of the skull. The whole time, Nefol's eyes had never left the snake.

She's good, thought Kirkgordon, but that snake's not going down so easily. And where the hell did they get it from?

Rising back into the air, the snake held itself some six feet off the ground and used its length to reach down and try to grab Nefol. She was avoiding the strikes but was struggling to connect with the beast's head. Kirkgordon looked into his quiver at the arrows he had taken from the manse basement, noting their different thickness and the markings on the flashings. They could have told me what each one is and what it does, he thought. Oh stuff it, the last one seemed alright, just pick one.

Nefol saw the arrow depart Kirkgordon's bow and screamed. She turned and ran away from the snake, heading towards one of the houses. The arrow buried itself in the beast, which began to hiss in anger. A small black hole appeared in the side of the animal, drawing in the rest of the creature with a sound like a child emptying the last dregs of juice through a straw. It folded in on itself for several seconds and then there was a silence. Kirkgordon was beginning to turn his back when he saw the hole erupt, spewing bits of snake all around with a thunderous cracking sound.

It was like getting caught in the spray of a muck spreader in the countryside, and it smelt just as bad. As he tried to straighten up, Nefol appeared, looking extremely angry.

"Why did you fire that one? They will have heard it. We need to go. And you need to lose your clothes. They won't miss the smell of the snake guts."

Kirkgordon was about to argue. He wanted to say that no one had told him what any of the arrows did. No one had given him a brief. No one had warned him about potential flying snakes. Oh, and actually, he had just sorted out their winged beast problem. But she was right. Well, she seemed to know as much as anybody about how this place and these ghostly creatures worked. So he stripped. Right down to his underpants. The crying man who had been looking out the window still looked out. He still had tears in his eyes. But he was now crying with laughter at the snake-splattered, near-naked warrior with bow and quiver strapped around him.

Nefol and Kirkgordon moved with haste away from the scene of the battle. Fortunately the air wasn't cold and so Kirkgordon felt physically comfortable with his new state of attire, if not emotionally. He felt he needed to address the issue of a nearly nude middle-aged man running around with a twelve-year-old girl fairly quickly. Nefol gave him a despairing stare and he asked if she was sure she wasn't already a teenager. Her tutted response only reinforced his suspicions.

Spotting a lone petrol station, Kirkgordon motioned that they should scout past it. From the outside there appeared to be no ghostly presence and Kirkgordon swept the interior swiftly but cautiously. After taking a moment to wash the snake guts out of his hair, it took Kirkgordon a full five minutes to find and dress himself in suitable clothing. The T-shirt he had found was a little large but at least the jeans were a close fit. Donning his quiver and bow, Kirkgordon emerged to find Nefol sitting with an iced drink from the automatic machine. Made from crushed ice with a syrup sauce running through it, it was one of those soft drinks that parents hate. Cheap and sugary – kids just love them. Maybe she was twelve after all.

Nefol didn't say much. Most directions were given with hand signals and Kirkgordon wasn't sure whether this was due to fear or a lack of connection with him. Without doubt she could fight – her dispatching of the ghosts had been impressive – but there still seemed to be a young girl in there.

They continued towards the care home, making their way through back gardens and alleys, trying to remain clear of the main roads. Looking over fences they saw more hybrid beasts. Beetles with fly wings, a wasp with legs, a seagull with crab pincers. Such a variety, but from where?

The other great difficulty was being seen by people in their houses who, trapped inside, would bang on the windows to raise attention. Given that neither Nefol nor Kirkgordon could enter the houses without becoming trapped themselves, remaining unseen was the best option.

The faces he saw haunted him, though. On passing one large bay window, Kirkgordon saw a young child who was yelling "Daddy" in a near scream. It cut at Kirkgordon. What if he never got home? How would his son feel? Or his daughter? And then there was Alana. He had damn well nearly slept with that other girl. And they say she's a witch. That was hard to believe. Maybe possessed a bit. Yes, maybe that.

He tried to bring the recent time spent with Alana and their children into view. The kids smiling as he rolled around the floor with them. Such a forgiving nature in them, thought Kirkgordon. But they have never seen me in the darkest times. Unlike their mother. Alana had tried, and they were as close as they had been in recent times, but still distant. Despite the moments spent in passion, they were still too far apart. A rift had been forged which neither Kirkgordon nor Alana had any idea how to bridge.

Nefol raised her hand and Kirkgordon halted his progress. They were some five hundred yards from the home and could see the entrance. Inside the front doors, Graham was sitting at the front desk. He was white and trembling. A number of ghostly deckhands were wandering around, laughing at him and teasing. Kirkgordon called Nefol back.

"The way I see it," whispered Kirkgordon, "is that you will

want to get that man out." Nefol nodded. "I thought so. His name is Graham. By the colour of him, he's not a willing party to this. But we don't know that, Nefol, so be careful and don't trust him. If we rescue him now, we won't have a chance to search the place properly as Havers requested. So we may well rescue one man but condemn us all to hell." He didn't want to lay this conundrum on the child but it was a matter of fact. "So here's my plan. You stay here and watch Graham. Don't do anything for thirty minutes. If I'm not back by then, rescue him and get away."

"But my father said I was to protect you. I cannot return without you," protested Nefol.

"That man in there" – Kirkgordon pointed at Graham – "is more important than me. You are now his protector. It's that simple. Don't worry about me. I have a quiver full of exploding arrows." Nefol smiled. She must think I'm a silly old fool, thought Kirkgordon. Oh well, at least she's with the plan.

Kirkgordon scouted round the outside of the care home looking for another entrance. At the rear of the building was a boiler house attached to the main building, complete with large chimney. All was quiet around it except for the hum of the boiler. This was the way, he decided. With pace, Kirkgordon crossed the concrete driveway that encircled the buildings and gently opened the boiler house door.

Inside was dark. No lights were evident so Kirkgordon left the door open very slightly, trying to let his eyes adjust to the lack of light. As he crouched, he became aware of some light breathing very close to him. He turned his head to the right and as his vision adjusted he made out two eyes looking directly at him. Then he felt a bony hand grab his wrist.

The Austerley Express

There's something dreadfully comical about all of this, thought Havers. Dressed in a loose-fitting robe with leggings made by wrapping material around his legs, he thought he should audition for the next sci-fi spectacular. On his hands were tight green gloves which matched the dark green slip-ons he was shod in. The overall khaki garb had been suggested by the priest and sourced from the basement. The arms and legs contained small rods, inserted during the wrapping process, meaning that any impact from them would hurt Captain Smith and his crew.

On an ancient Chinese highway, Havers might have been in his element, but these were the streets of the English coastal town of Dillingham. He was pushing a wheelchair. With a dull grey frame and a black leather seat, it was extremely modern, unlike its occupant. Slouching in the chair with a pair of machetes, albeit very special machetes, was the bulky, heavy-jowled bulldog, Mr Austerley. You'd think he could sit up properly.

Now at least, transporting the occult expert was getting easier. It had been a mile-long walk through the sewers with the overweight, single-footed hulk. But this was necessary and Havers had kept his professional exterior throughout. It's just his damn arrogance, thought Havers. I know this evil around me and I'm damn well respectful of it. But this fellow just charges in. Maybe Mr Kirkgordon's view is right. But needs must, and at the moment I need Mr Austerley, monoped though he is.

The old girl's doing alright though. He watched Jane Goodritch striding along beside him. All the way through the tunnels she hadn't complained or held back once. She's like a youth leader, Brown Owl showing the way. One of those ladies at the Women's Guild who manhandles the arrangements for fêtes. She shouldn't be here. This nonsense shouldn't happen to decent people. We're meant to keep them from it. I do the dirty work so they don't have to see any of it. And as for Mr Austerley insisting she had a weapon... Make her a threat and they won't focus on me. That's the trouble working with people like Mr Austerley, generating their own ideas, not following the department's well-drilled procedures. Mr Wilson wouldn't have made that mistake.

Wilson. The name hit him like the strike of a clanger on a bell. First a blunt strike, followed by a constant vibration to be chewed over by his mind. Havers was not prone to sentiment but Wilson had been a genuinely decent person. Many of his recruits were from tainted backgrounds with character flaws making them easy to cajole into this secret life. Few ever did the job willingly. Wilson did. Out of respect for the ordinary human. To protect the innocent. Havers remembered the initial interview well. And even as the world became a darker place, as Wilson became more involved in this strangeness they inhabited, his ideals remained. One day, he would have been Havers' successor. Havers was sure of it. Damn this job.

"Major Havers," said Jane Goodritch under her breath, "I

think I see something up ahead." They were in the middle of town and had so far evaded all of Captain Smith's crew. With a wheelchair occupant, one who could not even propel himself due to his ineptness with the device, and a middle-aged woman to defend, Havers had been banking on not meeting any resistance on his way to the museum. Although the crew was at least sixty strong, Dillingham was a moderately sized town and there should be plenty of hiding places.

The "thing" up ahead was at the junction of two streets. Their current route was taking them along a cobbled piece of the old town. The shops and abodes here were high and almost overhung the street, looming inward, or so it seemed to the walker beneath. Just a hundred yards ahead there was a side street and from here there emerged a long thin stick. Except it looked too flexible to be a stick. Almost like a giant feeler. Havers halted the party.

"Miss Goodritch," he whispered, "if you would be so kind as to take over. I know Mr Austerley is quite heavy but I believe you are a woman of talent and necessity and you may have to push quite quickly." Jane stepped across taking the handles of the wheelchair.

"Where to, Major Havers?" Havers wasn't sure.

"Forgive me, Miss Goodritch, just keep behind me."

Jane nodded. Up ahead, a second feeler was emerging as well as what appeared to be a black tusk.

"That's a beetle's tusk and a feeler. Lot bigger than you normally see though," said Austerley.

"You don't say, Mr Austerley," replied Havers. The full extent of the oversized insect became clear as several legs emerged and it turned the corner towards them. On its back was a scantily clad pirate with a cutlass in his hand. But most strange was the tail on the large beetle. Some five snakes emerged from its rear, attached by their tails to the beetle's body. The pirate saw his prey and kicked hard on the sides of the creature. It increased its pace, legs clicking forward like a clockwork machine.

"Behind me, Miss Goodritch," repeated Havers and set his face to the task ahead. Measuring up the beetle's attack, he began to run towards it. On reaching the creature, Havers jumped onto one of the tusks and grabbed a feeler, snapping it off. The pirate reached forward, swinging his cutlass. Havers ducked and the continuation of the swing took the blade through the other feeler. The creature threw its head up in pain and Havers was thrown off to the side. He landed on his side and turned his momentum into a roll but was instantly pinned by a set of fangs to the nearest wall.

Pain ripped through his shoulder and another snake head stabbed at his throat. Havers managed to get a blocking arm up but the snake bit into the arm and held on. A third snake head now grabbed his other shoulder. A fire raged through his body as Havers felt the venom being injected into him. His body tightened and he fought to keep moving. His upper frame was shutting down and he had no way to remove the snakes.

A blade cut through the snake holding his arm. Then the snake on his left shoulder went limp, followed by the one on the right. Jane Goodritch was standing beside him, waving one of Austerley's machetes at the remaining snakes which were striking towards her. One caught her on the shoulder but could not make a bite. The force knocked her backwards out of reach. Havers knew his time was short and forced his arms to lift. He ran at the beast again, dodging the snakes at its tail, and jumped onto the beetle's head. Stepping past a swinging cutlass, he dived head first at the pirate, causing them both to fall off the beetle. Havers recovered first. He wrapped his legs round the pirate and broke his neck.

"Mr Austerley, throw me the other machete!" ordered Havers.

Well back from the action, Austerley tossed his remaining blade, but Havers' paralysed arms failed to catch it. Come on, Arthur, Havers screamed internally, one last hurrah. He forced his right hand to close on the machete handle and picked it up.

The beetle had nearly reached Jane and the snake heads were stretching towards her. Havers ran to the back of the beetle and, in agony, forced his arms to stretch up and deliver a slicing blow to the base point from which the snakes emerged. They fell to the ground, writhing, and expired. Turning to the front of the beetle, Havers took several swings at the neck before the blade fell from his hand. The head was almost removed. It swung limply and the beetle collapsed, its legs giving way.

Havers sat on the ground, the world spinning around him as he fought for air. Sweat poured from his brow and what little sensation he still had in his upper body was fading. Jane hauled herself up from the ground and fought the terror racing through her.

What to do, she wondered. Think, woman, think!

Racing over to Havers, Jane grabbed at his top, pulling it back to reveal where the snake heads had bitten him. Placing her mouth over one of the wounds, she sucked at it then lifted her head to spit out what she had extracted. Jane continued this rapidly, drawing and spitting.

"Hurry up," hissed Austerley, "we don't know how many more of them there are around here."

"Shut up," spat Jane, "this man needs help." Austerley began to wheel himself away but his efforts were slow and stuttered.

"You wait there!" shouted Jane.

"Shush woman, you'll bring them running."

"Who cares? He saved us and now he needs help." Much to Austerley's disgust, Jane continued her workings and showed no sign of breaking off.

"Don't you think you've gotten most of it out by now?"

"I'm done when I'm done, Mr Austerley, and not a moment sooner!"

Looking around the tight street, Austerley saw no signs of movement except for the twitching death throes of the beetle creature. He shifted impatiently in his chair, waiting for Jane to finish.

"I think that's it. Time we were moving."

"Damn right. How exactly do you intend to get us out of here?" asked Austerley.

Well, thought Jane, there's only one obvious solution. "Time for you to hop along, Mr Austerley."

Looking at her as if she were mad, Austerley countered, "No way. I can barely stand without crutches and if something comes I'll be left behind. You'll not wait for me."

"Right enough, Mr Austerley. If you won't get out of the wheelchair, I'll use Plan B." Austerley watched in horror as Jane reached under Havers' arms and dragged him towards the wheelchair. As she got close, Jane lifted up Havers so that he was facing Austerley. Her own lack of height meant she was unable to extend Havers' legs fully and his knees were just above ground level.

"What are you going to do with him now?" enquired Austerley. Jane threw Havers on top of Austerley, who wasn't ready for him. Havers' head nutted Austerley and a stray knee lodged into Austerley's groin. Swearing out loud, he tried to push Havers back off him. Jane clipped him round the head and got behind the wheelchair.

"Do we still go to my museum?"

"Yes, yes, woman. Let's just get off the damn street so I can get rid of this lump on top of me." It took a moment to generate enough momentum for the stacked disability aid to start rolling. Once it started, Jane had no intention of stopping it. Austerley was pinned into the seat, hands holding on to the material at the back of Havers' legs, keeping them off the ground. He had no idea where they were or where the museum was. The town was generally quiet apart from the odd shout, yell or boisterous debate. Jane Goodritch had the sense to stay well clear of these sounds.

The rolling rescue passed a wide opening and Jane clocked two of Captain Smith's crew just off to her left. The gap to cross was too wide and she decided that she needed to turn around and find a different route. She halted her progress and tried to pull back on the wheelchair's handles, but her hands slipped off. She watched in horror as the wheelchair and its occupants sailed behind the crewmen before catching the pavement on the far side of the street and tipping over. Austerley was left face down, sprawled over Havers' body.

The two crewmen with their ghostly green glow turned around and strode over to the wheelchair disaster. Each drew his cutlass, pointing cautiously at the bodies on the ground.

"Do you think the boys are fooling with the dead again?" asked the first crewman.

"Doubt it. Something's up. Stick them and see if they're alive," answered the second.

The first crewman walked up cautiously and placed the

point of his weapon on the small of Austerley's back. He had, however, missed a few important details that had transpired during their conversation.

The fall had woken Havers up again. His arms were immobile, but his head and neck were free to move. A few whispered words in Austerley's ear had prompted the former professor to remove from Havers' jacket two very small darts and place them into Havers' mouth. And now, leaning over the prone bodies, the ghostly crewman presented a perfect target.

The second crewman saw his partner fall to the ground. Neither of the bodies had seemed to move.

"Stop messing about. We have patrolling to do. George, get up," said the second crewman. Striding over as he realized something was not quite right, there was the tiniest prick on his neck, feeling much like a midge bite. The crewman glanced briefly at the bodies before tumbling to the ground as his colleague's body faded to green mist.

"Not only my words are deadly but everything that comes from my mouth, Mr Austerley," croaked Havers. "Now, can you kindly get off me and get me back into the wheelchair? And Mr Austerley, kindly be more helpful to Miss Goodritch. She's doing jolly well considering she's never seen anything like this before. Jolly well indeed."

Museum Work

That's the door shut, Major Havers. Can I suggest we head deep inside the museum to avoid anyone catching sight of us?" suggested Jane Goodritch.

"Jolly well done, Miss Goodritch. I think I owe you my life. An excellent effort. Now the adrenalin is going to wear off, so be aware that you may feel some trauma or anxiety about what you have just gone through. Try to keep it at bay – we need your knowledge to assist Mr Austerley," advised Havers.

"Yes, Major Havers, I'll bear that in mind." Jane was sniffing as she spoke, her eyes reddening.

"And as for you, Mr Austerley, kindly get me a solution to all of this. So far you seem to be spending your time sat on that rather generous backside of yours. Pardon the expression, ma'am."

"I've lost a foot, Havers, don't you remember? I've lost a foot."

"We all suffer, Mr Austerley. Get on with it. Excuse the expression, but there's a bigger set of balls on Miss Goodritch here."

Austerley's face turned red with rage but Havers held his unusual expression, one of silent anger, before turning back to Jane.

"I suggest, Miss Goodritch, that you take Mr Austerley to your exhibits. Help him in whatever way he needs. And if you feel like smacking his backside because he makes some silly comment, then please show a little more professionalism than myself. I have a measured touch and can bring people excruciating pain without killing them. I fear your blow may be a little more brutal."

Austerley spat on the ground and hopped along the side of the wall. Opening the door marked "Exhibits" he made a show of turning his back on Havers and lifted his nose to the sky before his hopping action ruined the effect.

Havers turned to Miss Goodritch. "Apologies for that, but listen closely. That man is a genius in the matters that now confront us. Give him all the help you can, but make a note of what he says, for he is extremely unbalanced. I'm sorry but I am – Dillingham is – depending on you. I know that's a weight, believe me I know, but I believe fate has made a good choice this time."

"Fate alone does not make a choice, Major Havers. A choice implies a higher force influencing our actions. Picking a side."

"Ah, you are one of Mr Kirkgordon's kind. Good. And here," – Havers smiled – "call me Arthur. No one else does." She understands duty and she gets on with it, he thought. So like my mother. His mind filled with images of Russian snow and a stalwart woman refusing to break down despite immense torture. The confusion – hating her for abandoning him yet admiring her courage to save those who fought with her. All the worst times seem to be accompanied by snow. At least that was something for the here and now. No snow.

"I said Jane. Call me Jane."

"Sorry, my apologies, I was a little way away then. Jane, can you prop me up just across from the door? I should keep out of sight, and then I can deal with anything that comes our way."

"But you're paralysed. Your arms, they aren't going to function any time soon."

Havers smiled. "We are resourceful, Jane. I'm a little better trained for these things, but we are resourceful. Sort that damned fool out for me. I have something that might help."

Jane nodded, smiled back, and took something from him with a whispered instruction.

After positioning Havers as advised, Jane followed Austerley through the inner door. She found him looking around the Captain Smith exhibits.

"Not the greatest example of a museum I have seen," Austerley observed.

"And you're not the finest specimen of man I have seen either, but, like this collection, I guess you'll have to do. Shall we get down to it and stop throwing the childish insults?"

Austerley grunted and went back to reading the wall charts and looking at the various items in the collection. After ten minutes of silent observation he grunted again.

Without turning around, Austerley said, "Is there anything else to do with Smith? I mean, his story is pretty well covered, but one wonders where he got the idea to deal with the devil. Is there anything more about the bit... the woman, his woman... the witch?"

"Not in this room. We'll need to go into the back store. Maybe best if you go into the private observation room and I bring the items out."

"I can handle delicate items. I do have some experience of being in museums, delving into old books." Austerley flashed an angry look at Miss Goodritch.

"And you are missing a foot, Mr Austerley. Best that you rest and sit down to observe the items. Makes sense now, doesn't it?"

Austerley grunted and hopped along to a brown door indicated by Miss Goodritch. Inside he found a small table with a large lamp, which he switched on. Presently, he was joined by Miss Goodritch carrying several boxes.

"I think these will interest you, Mr Austerley. There's a book of tales about Captain Smith's woman – pretty lurid drawings, I'm afraid – a pendant dug up from the burial site of the captain, some town records about the altercation by the captain and his men. And there's this." Jane dropped a large battered manuscript onto the table. "It's a witch's journal, detailing her premonition..."

"Yes, I know what it is. A list of her descendants. Let me work, just let me work!" Austerley took the objects and placed them on the table. Taking the pendant in hand, he studied it carefully. It had a pentangle on it and was made of solid brass. "Where was the burial site?"

"I don't know, but I shall see what we have on the microfiche. The item was found some time ago, possibly a hundred years."

"A hundred? Are you sure?"

"Is your hearing deficient, Mr Austerley? I said I don't know, but if you will let me work..."

Austerley turned and saw two glowering eyes. He quickly resumed his studies. Satisfied that Austerley had understood her point, Miss Goodritch bustled away to the microfiche archives.

Austerley was making good progress with the items in front of him. Looking at the pentangle in detail, he could see that it was less than a hundred years old, so maybe witchcraft was still practised in the area. Exactly what sort, and its effects, would still need to be determined. The manuscript was more difficult to pin down. The language was old, very old, and most definitely not English.

In the beginning of his research into the darker things, Austerley would be poring over books, trying to decipher what was in them. Now he could read forty-three, no, forty-four ancient languages well and pronounce twenty-five of them: fifteen to a usable level and ten perfectly. And Kirkgordon can't even put on a French accent, he thought.

The overwhelming sense of pride he was building suddenly crashed down when he thought about his foot. At times he swore he could still feel it there, toes wriggling. It was also the foot that got coldest quickest, despite not being there. Bloody Farthington. And Churchy, pinning me to that board, trapped. Still, there were good reasons to have Churchy about. He was, after all, quite an inventive fighter.

Austerley's mind relived standing behind Kirkgordon as Farthington, in full dragon form, unleashed fire at them both. Churchy had got them out, had protected Austerley. The memory of the dragon's anger numbed Austerley to the core. He remembered looking into the depths of Dagon. Austerley's encounter with the demon had been his blackest moment on this journey.

Were the wondrous sights he had seen worth the ice he felt in his soul? The dreams were brutal and so vivid. But he was important, vital surely, or Havers wouldn't be entertaining him. Surely he was some sort of hero. Stopping Dillingham's descent into hell, being here now, fighting for restoration: all these things were in the plus column. How much to get into profit, though? And would his hunger for these things ever subside? Because he knew it was a hunger he could not control.

"I've checked the microfiche," said Miss Goodritch.

"That was quick. You said it would take a while," replied Austerley.

"I was two hours! Are you any further on?"

"No. She's a clever witch, whoever she was. But this is a common tongue for witches. Unholy and unknown to most folk, but not their most cryptic or contorted. Or blasphemous."

"And you can read all of these, Mr Austerley?"

"Oh, yes," said Austerley proudly. "I can read forty-five different occult languages. It takes a mind of discipline to do that."

"Takes a proud fool to see that as compensation for a missing foot. You should have tried table tennis."

"Table tennis?"

"Yes. Very few people lose their foot playing the old ping-pong. Might even have got you back into shape. You really are quite fat."

Austerley looked over Miss Goodritch's ample, rotund figure, making a show of it so that she would get his point.

"Two grown men, a wheelchair and three dead snakes. It was this fat ass that saved your fatter ass, Mr Austerley. Don't insult those looking after you. For a man with such brains, you really are quite the imbecile."

Austerley raised his eyebrows and shook his head. "Did you find the burial site?"

"The care home. It was built about thirty years ago. Before that there was a cinema. And before that, approximately one hundred years ago, it was a burial site. Now, I'm going to see if the useful man needs anything." Miss Goodritch turned with aplomb and started to walk away.

"Miss Goodritch!"

"Yes?"

"Thank you. And for your services earlier too."

"You're welcome, Mr Austerley." And with that she was gone.

Austerley wondered. If they were buried there, why was the hill being used to restore the captain? It made no sense. Unless they buried them separately. Unless the captain isn't the real thing. This is wrong, Austerley. The captain, if he had made a deal, wouldn't be looking to descend into hell. He would want to reign above ground. Why leave one world to visit another and then come back? This was wrong.

Austerley stood up on his good leg and began hopping out to the entrance foyer of the museum. Havers would have an idea. Austerley needed to talk with someone who understood these matters, to compare notes, to see if his thinking was on the right lines about the missing evidence. Havers was an expert in deception and subterfuge. He'd see the bluff if it was there.

Austerley pushed the door open and then remembered the foyer had a glass front that could be seen from the street. Havers would be pissed at him for just wildly walking out there. Oh well, done now. Austerley scanned the foyer looking for whichever hidey-hole Havers was occupying. But there was no one.

"Havers? Havers, are you there? It's important, I need to run some things past you. Havers? Miss Goodritch? Are you there?" There was no response. Austerley hopped back through the door and began to call out for Miss Goodritch, fearing she had crossed behind him earlier and he had missed her. But there was no reply. Austerley continued to search until the effort of hopping around exhausted him and he had to sit down.

It was so small that Austerley had missed it several times

before he finally saw it. The tiny token lying on the floor had writing on it. Austerley recognized the language as one first discovered in the Antarctic mountains but never revealed to the general public. It read, as best as he could approximate, "my little world". Maybe "my place to hide". Either way, he knew what it did. It shielded the person inside a different plane, removing them and the space around them to an out-of-sight spot between the dimensions.

He had been hidden. Whatever had happened to Havers and Miss Goodritch, they were elsewhere. And now he was on his own, seriously impeded in his mobility and an easy target should anyone come past. It had been a long time since he had been in danger on his own and he didn't like it one bit.

Austerley Meets His Match

Austerley hopped back to his previous seat to contemplate what he should do. *I'm not buying this current idea of Captain Smith coming back to take over,* he thought. *This is something different. The witch seems to be the key to it all. All the symbolism I've found points to her. But why do all this? Why have a charade? When I stopped this place from falling into hell, it seemed… easy. Even though I was drained and doped. I'm sure I couldn't have been in a frame of mind to react with accuracy, so why let me think so? They tried to kill Havers, so he can't have been part of the plan. Unless his death was. And why is the witch targeting Churchy? She's going at his weakness, his libido. Why him? Something is not right. The conjoined animals, where did they come from? That's not witch magic. She could have summoned creatures, shadows and faeries, but not built her own. Something is wrong. This is all subterfuge. Definitely a cover-up, but why? And if we are not in the realms of hell then where are we?*

Austerley froze in his seat as the front door of the museum opened, the little bell tinkling its acknowledgement. Whoever had come in was making very little noise. *Damn this foot,* thought Austerley, *I'll be like a clanging bell if I start to hop.* Then, in what clever people often mistake to be practical wisdom, Austerley lay on the floor so that he could move along quietly by dragging himself. Slowly, he hauled himself across the floor towards the door that led to the foyer. One more drag and he would be able to look through the small window-slits and see who was there.

The door opened and cracked Austerley on the skull. Rolling over, Austerley groaned before looking up into the face of a ghoulish deckhand. It laughed and punched him on the head, sending a driving pain through Austerley's brain. His eyes began to water.

"He wants you," said the deckhand. "Specifically asked for you. Says the captain ain't getting his hands on the prize. You'd be better off with the captain, laddie. You sure know how to piss off the wrong—"

The rest of his words were sent to oblivion as a machete bit into his neck. The deckhand fell and faded into a green gas. Austerley looked up into the eyes of a familiar force of nature.

"Where is Major Havers? And why are you rolling around on the floor?" asked a rather cross Miss Goodritch. "Where have you been? I was just walking around here and then you were gone. Major Havers said to drop a little token behind you after I had seen him and that was the last I saw of you. He gave me one too, and told me to get back to looking for more items. I come back out and you are rolling around on the floor like an idiot with one of those ghouls over you."

"Long-dead spirit, actually, with no real earthly existence."

"Don't you start that mumbo-jumbo with me, Mr Austerley. Lucky that Major Havers told me to take this knife with me."

"Machete."

"What?"

"Machete. It's a machete. Not a knife. It's not from a

kitchen.”

"Enough of your cheek, Mr Austerley. Now tell me what is going on."

Austerley looked at the woman standing above him. She had a solid frame and looked like a hospital matron. Forthright actions and a lack of panic had built her reputation, but right now she was shaking. Tears began to stream down her face and the machete dropped from her hands, missing Austerley's face by a few centimetres.

"How could Major Havers leave us like this? We need him to protect us, to tell us how to deal with these things."

"It's okay, Miss Goodritch, I'm here."

Miss Goodritch looked straight at Austerley lying on the floor, barely able to sit up and started to laugh. It was a hysterical laugh, born of desperation – the last defence before succumbing to the madness. She sniffed occasionally as she roared, hauling back her decency with rasping snorts.

Austerley felt pathetic. Unsure if he had enough strength to stand up, he was unable to comfort Miss Goodritch with his actions, and his words were obviously not required at this time.

Miss Goodritch composed herself. "So where is Major Havers? Why did he leave us, and how?"

"I think he was attacked, Miss Goodritch, and I think he knew it was coming."

"What do you mean?"

"Well, that token he gave you opened up a parallel plane for me to exist in. It's damn difficult to see unless you have a trained eye. Basically, I am here but not in the same dimension. I think the theory comes from a Swiss philosopher from the sixteenth century who had a rather dubious reputation for using drugs and animal blood to expand his mind. His name was—"

"I don't care what his bloody name was," roared Miss Goodritch. "Where is Major Havers?"

"They have him, I think," said Austerley quietly. "He gave us these shelters to protect us. And he's either with them or he's..."

"Dead. Just say it. I can take it." Jane sat down on the floor. "No time for this now, Mr Austerley. What do we do?"

"I'm not sure. I'm really not sure."

An Old Friend Checks In

Flicking his head out of the door, Kirkgordon saw two deckhands surrounded by their green aura. They were agitated, probably by the raucous sound made by the carnage that the black hole in the basement had caused. Pulling all of his arrows out of the quiver, Kirkgordon tried to assess which were the least potent. All the arrows looked the same except for the flashings on the ends. Although the feathers were of the same size, there was a myriad of colours. Behind him, he could hear Tania moving again, picking herself off the floor. Oh well, he thought, let's see what this one does.

Kirkgordon kicked open the door and fired an arrow into the back of the nearest ghost. A massive hand, five feet in diameter, appeared out of nowhere and picked up the ghoul. The next moments were a blur of green as the hand slammed the ghost into the ground on the left and then the right, possibly ten to fifteen times in a few seconds. By the time the other ghost had turned, he had received an arrow in his chest and instantly exploded, his body parts then dissolving into the green gas Kirkgordon had seen before.

Racing along the corridor, Kirkgordon dived into a room as more ghosts turned the corner ahead. An old man was lying on the bed in his dressing gown. In many ways he was rather dapper except that his right eye was closed over – scarred, in fact – with no hint of eyelashes. There was just a series of stitches where the eyeball should have been located.

"Trouble, old bean?" asked the patient.

"Stay there and don't move. If they look in I won't be here," replied Kirkgordon.

"It's okay, they're all perfectly friendly. Splendid company for a G & T."

The voice sounded familiar to Kirkgordon. Despite the threat from the ghosts in the corridor, Kirkgordon stood just inside the doorway and stared at the man. No, he thought, it can't be. The height is right and the body shape too. The voice is Havers to a tee, but... the left eye, that stare. Windows to the soul. A soul that looks dark from here. Very dark, and full of vengeance. And it was the right eye that I hit. Could it be...?

A ghost turned into the room and, seeing Kirkgordon, started to draw its cutlass. Given the unpredictable close-range effects of his arrows, Kirkgordon slapped his bow across the ghost's head, causing the ghost to fall to the ground. Stepping over it and out of the door, Kirkgordon fired an arrow down the corridor into the midst of a group of deckhands. From nowhere, a one-eyed giant with a large wooden club appeared and began beating the deckhands to a pulp. Green bodies flew in all directions, flattening against the walls of the corridor.

Despite the wondrous and brutal sight ahead, Kirkgordon turned his head back to the old man lying on the bed. The man was smiling fiendishly.

"Tell Austerley I'll be seeing him soon, looking for his other foot," the man stated calmly. "It's time he learned to grovel on his knees."

Kirkgordon froze at the voice, so many memories flooding

back. His arm twitched as he remembered drawing his bow with a broken arm, the pain coursing through him.

"And as for you, Kirkgordon, your good book does say 'an eye for an eye', does it not?"

Farthington! How did Farthington get into the middle of this?

Kirkgordon did not wait to engage Farthington but fled the room and ran towards his one-eyed giant. The corridor was clear of ghosts and the creature, rippling with enormous muscles and sporting golden locks that reached far down his back, knelt before Kirkgordon's approach.

"Master," said the creature, in a voice that was two octaves below the bass scale, "what is your wish?"

Now, thought Kirkgordon, this is more like it! "Ahead! For the front door. And wipe the floor with anything green," ordered Kirkgordon, waiting for the creature to take the lead. The pair pounded down the corridor, which was clear down to the right-angled corner at the end. Kirkgordon waited and let the creature turn the corner alone. There was a wild roar from the giant, like the worst pealing of thunder, before a silence broke. Kirkgordon juked round to see the giant on his knees, wiping the carpet with a ghost in each hand. Much to the giant's disgust, the ghosts soon turned into green gas and disappeared. He looked again at his master.

"On," shouted Kirkgordon.

Just ahead was the front desk. Kirkgordon could see Graham sitting petrified with a number of ghosts before him. His face became a mask of bemusement when he saw the approaching giant. Pulling himself from the sight, Graham dived under his desk. Kirkgordon was a few steps behind the giant and he let the creature engage the ghosts. There was little style to the creature's bludgeoning actions but his sheer power was unmatched by the deckhands, who quickly capitulated to his maiming club. Within ten seconds there was only a dissipating mass of green gas to indicate that the ghosts had ever been present.

"I see you have your pets too."

Tania's voice. Kirkgordon looked for her and was amazed to see her appear, in naked form, from thin air beside the giant. Raising her left arm, she slowly closed her fist while staring at the giant creature, which collapsed in on itself before vanishing altogether. Kirkgordon, despite having only known his ally for a few minutes, was shocked at his disposal.

On hearing Tania's voice, Graham raised his head above the desk. Kirkgordon watched him drink in her form, drooling slightly despite the wild scenario he found himself in. She extended one hand and with a solitary finger beckoned Graham to come to her. Like a strutting peacock she arched her back, displaying her ample womanly charms, and Graham advanced, caught on her sexual hook. His mind filled with every dream he had ever had about her, and she seemed ready to play them all out.

"Graham! Grahamsey, snap out of it! She'll kill you!"

Graham continued to advance.

"Whatever depravity you can imagine, you can experience with me. Come to me now, Graham, and feast on me!" Graham broke into a run and fell at her feet. Starting at her thighs, Graham indulged in her flesh, taking less than a minute to reach her mouth, hands exploring with wild abandon. He's in a trance, thought Kirkgordon. Tania grinned at Kirkgordon between moments of sexual pleasure.

"Spurn me, Churchy? Turn me down, the finest flesh you

could ever taste? Then I will indulge in every other male and bring them to their knees." She took Graham by the back of the neck and engaged his mouth in a brutal kiss before pulling him by the neck to his knees. She raised her other arm and Kirkgordon watched her nails grow until they looked like four little blades. Pulling Graham's head back, she exposed his neck and Kirkgordon saw that her next action would be to slash Graham's throat. He drew the bow quickly and uttered one word.

"Stop!"

"You won't. You don't even know what those arrows do. Don't bluff me."

Kirkgordon let the arrow go. His target was a mere ten feet away and the arrow flew true, only to be caught in Tania's hand.

"Ha—" Tania was interrupted by a devastating series of blows from Kirkgordon's bow which battered her to the ground. Stooping over her, Kirkgordon made sure she was out cold. Graham was reeling on the ground.

"Are you okay?" asked Kirkgordon.

"Was she...? Did I just...? Wow. Why did you do that to her? She was letting me loose on her. Four months I have wanted her. God, she's beautiful. And naked, just for me."

"Snap out of it. She's a witch and she was going to cut your throat. Now, get your arse out of here, through the front door. There's a twelve-year-old girl who'll help you." It occurred to Kirkgordon that this was not the most enticing idea of safety, so he grabbed Graham by the collar, pointed him to the door and kicked his backside, yelling at him to move. Before Graham had reached the door, Nefol was already there.

"Get him out of here," ordered Kirkgordon. "Is there a car anywhere near? We really need to go quickly."

Nefol nodded. "Red one, far side of the car park. I'll get it started."

Damn, she is enterprising for a young one, thought Kirkgordon. He looked at Tania on the ground. Graham was right, she was stunning. How could something so beautiful be so evil? How could he hunger for something so dangerous? And then pity overtook him. A part of it must surely have been internal, but there was a serenity about Tania that made him think of her welfare, her protection. Havers would have a dizzy fit, but damn it. What had the priest said? I'm not one of his cronies. Sorry, Alana, but I've got to bring a naked woman back to my digs.

Kirkgordon grabbed Tania and lifted her up. He tried to ignore her figure as it slid over his face and then over his shoulder. This was dangerous. Was she really worth the risk? Surely we all are, he thought. "Are You watching?" he shouted to the heavens. "You taught me this, it's your fault." With one hand on her naked bottom for support and her glorious legs bouncing along in front of him, Kirkgordon raced out of the care home and over to the red car.

Nefol was in the driver's seat with Graham sitting in the rear, shaking. The car was extremely small and would be tight transport for four. Kirkgordon opened the front passenger door and carefully manoeuvred Tania and himself into the front seat. He had to turn her somewhat and she ended up sitting on his lap, her head on his shoulder, lolling about. Nefol shook her head.

"Don't give me that. You're twelve, and you don't understand!" shouted Kirkgordon. "Get the car started."

"It is," came the sarcastic reply.

It dawned on Kirkgordon that the car was electric. It made

little noise as it moved out of the car park. Clever girl, he thought, silent through the town, attracting little attention. Then he thought, she's twelve, how the hell's she driving?

As the adrenalin started to ease he thought about Farthington and his threats. There won't be an easy way out, that swine will have set something up good.

"Nefol, step on it. We need to make sure Austerley's safe. I just saw Farthington."

She looked at him like he was daft. "Who's that?" She had been spared meeting him. Well that's good, he thought.

"Zmey Gorynych."

"Oh, the Russian dragon."

She's too clever by half, this one, he reckoned. Tania moaned slightly and seemed to stir. Squeezing the pressure point in her neck, he watched her facial expression collapse to a deep peace again.

"Drive, Nefol, drive." He looked out the window at the sea with its horizon of fire and wondered what to do next. "Just drive. Let's hope Havers and your father know what to do."

The Redoubtable Miss Goodritch

We can't just sit here, Mr Austerley, we need to do something."

"Miss Goodritch, what exactly would you have us do? I'm a cripple and you're just a girl guide with a diploma in history." Austerley felt a hand clip him round the head.

"I'm the girl guide who saved you while you sat trying to wheel yourself out of the mess we were in. When it comes to looking after us, I think you'll find you are without doubt the weaker subject."

After opening his mouth to say something, Austerley found himself shutting it again without a sound. She was right and it pissed him off completely.

"Listen," said Austerley after a few moments of silence, "we are in a precarious position. But there's also something else going on which I can't figure out just now. I don't think this is about Dillingham at all. I think it's about Kirkgordon and me, possibly Havers too. Somebody has gathered us together. The history and witchcraft don't add up. There's a lack of continuity in what's happening. And these creatures that are a jumbled up mesh of animal parts, why are they here? If we descended to hell there would be no need for them – there would be demons aplenty to contend with. No, this is wrong, Miss Goodritch, plain wrong."

"Well, what do you need to figure it out, Mr Austerley? Major Havers said you were a genius at this kind of thing. So tell me what you need and I'll get it for you."

"You sound very like him. If they want me, then it's best for me to stay hidden. There are things in my head that could be used against the world itself. You may look surprised, but it has happened before." Austerley thought of Dagon rising on that Scottish island and a cold shiver ran through him. He had been one drug-induced moment from dooming the world. And bloody Churchy had shot him in the foot.

"But I don't need to stay hidden, so what can I do?" Miss Goodritch's face looked grim and slightly scared. Austerley wondered if Havers was like this underneath with a professional face on top.

"Two things, Miss Goodritch, two things. I need a piece of one of the creatures. There are certain chants I can perform to ascertain who really created them. And if I know that, I can assess their true power. Also, for some reason the hill top, Gibbet Point, is important. I'll need a piece of ground from there and a selection of herbs and liquids. Do you have a DIY shop and a herbalist in this town?"

"Yes, not far, either. But they may be protected by Father Jonah. If I go in then I won't be able to get out."

"No, but someone might be inside. Do they have live-in quarters above them?"

"Herbalist, yes, but not the DIY place, it's quite large," said Miss Goodritch.

Austerley thought for a moment. "Then the DIY store shouldn't be protected. The priest wouldn't dilute his power unnecessarily. But the herbalist more than likely will be."

"Well, I know Alan Hamley. If he's inside I may be able to communicate with him. Can things be passed out? Or are they trapped like people?"

"Father Jonah never said, Miss Goodritch, so that's going to have to be a chance we take."

After excusing herself to perform her ablutions, Jane Goodritch returned and picked up the remaining machete. Austerley had heard her throwing up but declined to comment. A strange feeling of sympathy formed inside him but he drove it back down, happy in the knowledge he was going to sit in his interdimensional hideaway.

"Give me two hours, Mr Austerley, and then consider me lost."

Shaking off the image of a Second World War film, Austerley nodded and watched the plump figure disappear through the doors of the museum. He cursed Havers' name, wondering at how the government man could have got himself caught. Some bloody professional he is.

Meanwhile, Jane stepped back out to the street, her head constantly on the move, eyeing every doorway. All was quiet as she walked stealthily along the road. After a few steps she broke back into her normal gait, deciding she might as well be comfortable in her walk. It wasn't as if she would be outrunning anything that appeared on the journey.

She fought hard against the image of Havers under torture. Her protector had been brave, sending her to safety despite his incapacitation. Tears started to form as she thought of him suffering at the hands of these ghosts and these awful creatures. She pulled Austerley's ingredients list from her pocket and forced herself to read through it to steady her nerves.

Look at the names, she thought. How was she meant to spot

these things? Chemical after chemical and even a few formulae to contend with. She was a museum curator, not a chemist. The man was such a clown. Don't worry, Miss Goodritch, it's all down there. No point turning back now, though. She had walked halfway there already so she might as well continue and hope for the best.

The walk through the next few streets was quiet. She passed by various windows and saw frightened people looking out from behind the blinds. There were faces she recognized from the museum, customers but not acquaintances. Knowing these people were safe brought her some relief. She tried to focus on this fact and ignore the present danger.

The DIY store looked deserted. It had been night-time when the attack had happened and no one had been shopping then. Approaching the doors, she was surprised when they slid apart. Surely they should still be on the overnight security settings? She swallowed hard and clutched her machete tighter, stepping gingerly into the store.

The moderately sized store had seven aisles packed with various household and DIY items. Tins of paint, chemical treatments, kitchenware, gardening accessories, lighting and other everyday requirements of the Dillingham handyman were catered for in abundance. But somewhere amongst all of the items was an intruder, maybe even more than one. The thought chilled Jane; she had been building up the notion that she could handle a single ghost, but not a horde.

From her vantage point at the entrance she looked around the store but was unable to see anyone. However, the store design was such that most of the building was beyond her range of vision. She took a trolley and, pushing it with her left hand, machete held in the right, she started her strange shopping trip.

Bang! The sound reverberated around the store. In her haste to get started, Jane had clipped a pyramid of tinned varnish with her trolley and it had collapsed, tins tumbling to the ground. She waited for a reaction, not flinching. After a few moments, she realized the stupidity of this tactic and ran with the trolley into the first aisle. At least here she was hidden from some eighty percent of the store. Clutching the machete in front of her, Jane anxiously watched for any sign of movement at either end of her aisle, her head snapping back and forward like she was sat watching a tennis match. But nothing moved.

After holding her ground for two minutes, Jane decided to proceed and took out the list she had written of the items Austerley had requested. Some of the items were easy to find, like the paint thinners. Austerley also wanted some bowls and tumblers, and the kitchenware aisle provided these. There was one word written out by Austerley himself as Jane couldn't begin to spell what he had said. Calcium hexadi-something-or-other. There was no tub or box with that label, and Jane began to examine the ingredients lists for the compound. After thirty minutes of fruitless searching for the exact name she began to put in any item with a vague connection to the name. He'll just have to make do, she thought.

Having collected all the items she could from the shelves, Jane pushed her trolley to the front of the store and noticed something across the door. A spider's web had formed, completely blocking the entrance. Something had been in here... no, something was still in here. Jane looked around for another exit. Her trolley was full, and she required a flat exit if her shopping trip was not to be in vain.

Surely, she thought, with the size of the items in here there must be a flat way out to the loading bay. Jane grabbed her trolley and pushed it briskly to the rear of the store. In order to keep panic at bay, practicality took charge, and all her thought processes worked on what she had to do. This prevented any thought of what might be waiting. She really didn't like spiders. Not one bit.

On reaching the rear of the store, she cautiously poked her head through some plastic curtains – the strip type allowing access but cutting out any drafts – and all was quiet so she hauled her trolley through the flexible barrier and looked for an exit. This part of the building was like a warehouse. Great cardboard boxes on pallets filled large sections of racking that had been laid out so that the pallets could be easily moved around.

Jane stopped. She listened. Her heart started to beat faster as she heard the faintest of movements. She strained to ascertain its direction. Hell, that's behind me. She ran.

Jane and her trolley, wheels spinning fast, rounded the racking at the end of the corridor and almost crashed. With every muscle, she pulled back and stopped herself and the trolley from piling into the abomination ahead. For the briefest of moments her curiosity outweighed her fear and she inspected the nightmare before her.

There was a spider at its core, of that there was no doubt. But it was larger than any spider Jane could ever have imagined. Eight legs jutted out from its sides without meeting the floor, and another set of legs emerged from underneath the body; each was thin with three appendages at the end, like the leg of a robin. And from its centre, above the spider's fangs and eyes, jutted out the head of a lizard. The whole mish-mash of animals was ten feet tall and Jane was taken aback by the vulgarity of the experiment. She fled, without her trolley, machete in hand.

In a state of panic, the mind will reach for the option that indicates the greatest safety. Jane was now in a full panic. She began to run around the warehouse, passing through small gaps in the racking, forcing the creature to take the longer route. Running was not a pastime Jane was well acquainted with and she soon ran out of breath. As she slowed down she felt the creature getting closer with each corner. Soon her lungs were gasping for air and she felt nauseous. She tripped and fell into the middle of a corridor. She looked up to see the creature hopping like a robin around the corner. Its fangs were showing. The teeth on the lizard's head were gleaming, and there was malice in its eyes. Overcome by sheer terror, she vomited heavily onto the floor.

The bird legs folded up underneath the animal and it scuttled forward on its spider's legs. As it rose up before her, Jane saw its fangs and, beyond that, a sharp implement. She realized that the weapon of capture was a paralysing spear, a spider's stinger. As the appendage began to move, she covered her face with her hands and waited for her end.

Back From The Dead

They say that your life flashes before your eyes at the end. Jane Goodritch had no time to contemplate this as she watched a rapid movie of her days so far. Her happy parents playing with her at the beach, her grandmother's funeral, her history award in secondary school, the death of her first boyfriend by a hit and run driver (an event which had kept her single since), winning the post of museum curator: all raced before her. And then the underside of the creature came back into view to terrify her one last time. So it ended like this.

The gunshot made her jump. And the second one. She heard a clicking sound followed by two more shots. Then she heard scuttling and opened her eyes to an empty corridor with no conglomerated creature in sight. Her body was overcome with relief and she started to cry loudly, the tension of the previous moments catching up with her.

"I wouldn't sit there, ma'am. If you'll walk towards my voice, I'll be able to fend off that thing if it comes back."

The voice was from the north of England, but the wording was precise and almost masked the accent. Maybe Cumbria, she thought, before shaking her mind and body into action. Jane walked backwards to the voice, keeping her eyes peeled for the spider creature.

"There's an office behind us. The door is strong and has kept that creature from me since I got here. We'll go inside and you can tell me what you've been shopping for."

Jane could feel her breathing slow down with the calmness of the voice, and apart from the sick taste in her throat she felt strong again. Turning around, she saw a man standing in an office doorway with a shotgun in his hand. Jane started to ask a question.

"Not at the moment, ma'am," interrupted the man, "let's get inside the office first, shall we? There are no guarantees with creatures like that taking their fill of the place."

Jane obliged and walked past the man into the office. Dressed in black leggings and a black top, he cut quite a figure, but there was something in his demeanour that reminded her of someone. She couldn't quite place the similarity but she did feel safer with him around.

Once they were both inside with the door locked behind them, the man pulled over a chair and offered it to Jane. She saw that he had several severe cuts and his top was soaked with blood.

"You look in a bad way," Jane said, waiting for an explanation.

"Yes, I do, don't I. Sorry about that. Allow me to introduce myself. The name's Wilson. And whom did I have the pleasure of rescuing?"

"Jane Goodritch, Mr Wilson. That's right isn't it? Wilson's your surname."

"Yes. My surname. What made you think that?"

"You have a way of speaking. I have a friend who speaks like you. Well, maybe had..." Jane broke into tears and Wilson stepped forward and bent down for her to cry on his shoulder. As she sobbed, she realized that Mr Wilson smelt dreadful.

Maybe it was the congealed blood, but she thought there was the smell of mud and dirt there too.

Jane's curiosity forced her to muffle her cries. Sniffing hard, she found herself able to ask a question. "What on earth happened to you?"

"Nothing much, really. First, let's see what happened to you. I saw you enter the shop on the cameras over here. Rather a bizarre little shopping trip. The recent turn of events has deterred most from the summer sales."

His manner was polite but searching. She felt that he was saying: I will have my answers but we can be civilized about it if you wish, or otherwise if there's trouble. And getting the chair, very chivalrous. Of course. Arthur.

"Do you know Arthur?"

The man cocked an eyebrow. "Any particular brand of Arthur or just the common garden variety?" His grin was soft, easing her nerves, like Arthur. The man was also dapper like Arthur, but younger, maybe late twenties at most. His hard edge was concealed so well that Jane had nearly forgotten how he had handled a shotgun. Surely he knew Arthur.

"Arthur Havers. A friend of mine. Very practical man."

Wilson barely flinched. But he was staring at her now like he had her under a microscope trying to determine some truth about her.

"How do you know Major Havers?" The tone was serious and even. After the previous friendly voice, this indicated a more professional urge.

"I was helping him. We were on our way to my museum when we were attacked by some kind of beetle monster and Arthur, sorry, Major Havers, was bitten by snakes. He was paralysed, his arms, so I took him and Mr Austerley to my museum. While we were there he hid us, and then we think he was taken by these ghosts. Now I'm collecting some items for Mr Austerley so that we can find out what's happened to Arthur."

"Mr Austerley's here?" Wilson was suddenly right in front of Jane's face. "Where?"

"At the museum. He's a cripple and..."

"Yes, I know about the foot, Farthington took it from him. Is he alone in the museum?"

"Yes, I left him there to come and get the stuff he asked for."

"But they'll get him! You know what Mr Austerley is, don't you?"

"No. Apart from a grumpy old man with a missing foot and a penchant for the occult."

"It's not a hobby, Miss Goodritch, he's probably the fore-most... did you say old?"

"Yes, he must be in his eighties."

"Damn, they got to him. He won't last. They were all dying at the care home."

"The care home. Mr Kirkgordon went there. With the priest's daughter."

"Nefol with Mr Kirkgordon? I need to know everything, Miss Goodritch, and I need to know fast, because we have to get to Mr Austerley right away and protect him."

"He's safe, Mr Wilson." Jane explained all that she knew to Wilson, including the secret hiding dimension Havers had set up for Austerley and herself. Kneeling in front of her, Wilson listened attentively, his face utter concentration. Jane was sure there was an engine running on full behind it. When she had finished speaking, he drew away for a short moment before turning back.

"Mr Austerley seems to believe that these ingredients are

required, so I think we should pick up the remaining items and get back to him. I don't like the idea of you all running around in the open, so when we get to the museum it may be best to put you in a sanctuary with Mr Austerley and I will fetch the priest and Mr Kirkgordon. Are you up to walking?"

"Yes, thank you. I feel better now."

"And I'll take your machete. Not that it will do much good against the ghosts."

"Oh, it works on them. The priest has a vault of weapons, apparently. Arthur brought this with him. This one and another. He still has that, I hope."

"Good," said Wilson, scanning the cameras. "That spider thing is in the top far corner of the warehouse, so stay quiet and then hopefully we can sneak out with the goods."

Jane watched Wilson check the shotgun, making sure it was loaded.

"Do you have many more shots?"

"Just what's loaded, ma'am. Still, stiff upper lip."

Jane's renewed vigour took a hit. Then a thought crossed her mind. "Mr Wilson. How did you get here? I have told you everything I know and have got nothing from you. How do I know you aren't on their side? How do I know I'm not about to lead you straight to Mr Austerley as a hostage?"

"Very good, Miss Goodritch. Major Havers doesn't choose his allies lightly. You have also handed me your only weapon. Not smart at all, but at least you got there in the end. All you have is my knowledge of your companions, my saving you from that spider and a little bit of trust. It's very hard in our game, trust. Yet it is what keeps you alive, well, until you trust the wrong person. I work for Major Havers. I was his original man here in Dillingham, sent after the priest contacted him about some strange occurrences. But trust is all I can offer, Miss Goodritch. Let's hope it's enough." Wilson walked to the door and opened it. "Shall we?"

Jane stood up and followed Wilson out into the warehouse. They could see the giant creature in the far corner of the room. It moved up onto its bird legs.

"He's seen us," said Wilson in a hushed tone. "Just walk calmly and quickly towards the trolley. I want you to push it. I'll need to be free to defend us."

Jane nodded and followed Wilson towards the trolley. The spider began to strut towards the trolley from the other side of the warehouse. On reaching proximity, the spider dropped back to its spider legs and scuttled to within ten metres. Jane had just reached the trolley when the creature started stalking forward, approaching slowly.

"The door behind me, Miss Goodritch. There's a ramp beyond. Don't wait for me."

Jane turned the trolley and walked briskly for the door. She heard two shots and then Wilson cried out and something solid clattered into the racks. Breaking into a run, she was forced to halt abruptly as the spider dropped down from the racks above and blocked her path to the door. Terror struck her, and her protector was nowhere to be seen. The spider crept forward and its fangs moved ever so slightly. Jane retreated, but the spider kept closing in. She was transfixed by its evil-looking mouth and eyes, and as it rose up to reveal once more its puncturing, paralysis-inducing limb, she nearly fainted. Surely, this time she was finished.

A splash of liquid fell onto the spider from above. Several drums, high up on the racking, were on their side with their contents pouring out onto the beast. A human figure, difficult to perceive in the darkness of the roof, was igniting a small firework with some matches. The fuse fizzed and the firework fell. Before the spider could react, the liquid caught fire and the creature began to thrash in pain.

Jane turned on her heel and ran with the trolley towards the nearest door. She turned the handle and opened the door, pushing the trolley through into better light. There was a ramp down to the lorry park behind the building. She made for one of the large refuse containers and hid both herself and her goods behind it. With her heart pounding and at her wits end, she shuddered violently, the shock hitting her body with a vengeance. She felt a tap on the shoulder and tried to scream, but a hand clapped over her mouth before the sound could leave. Her head turned to see this new threat. She found herself looking at a smiling Wilson.

"Hold this," he said, handing over the machete. "I think I've broken a finger."

Jane took hold of the weapon and watched as Wilson took some tape from his pocket and taped his middle and ring fingers together.

"Are you okay?" asked Jane.

"Yes, but we need to move. I couldn't stop the fire spreading. I imagine there will soon be investigations from parties we won't appreciate. Time to go, Miss Goodritch. Time to go."

Team Austerley

Austerley was annoyed. Jane had said she would be back in two hours and it was now an hour and a half since she had left. Technically she wasn't late and he had no right to complain, but he desperately wanted those items. His deductions were complete and he needed the items to proceed further with his investigation. It also bothered him that he was skulking away in another dimension while a plump, middle-aged woman was leading the fight. Although Austerley's passion for self-preservation was undiminished, his ego was taking a full broadside at this turn of events.

Anyway, thought Austerley, I need a leak, and Havers didn't put a port-a-potty in this caravanette. The wonders of inter-spacial dimensions and the absurdity of being somewhere and yet not being there weren't unnoticed by Austerley, but he had seen so many weird, wonderful and abhorrent sights that basic human functions had begun to outweigh them.

Hopping across the corridor to the door with the little man on it, Austerley entered and decided to sit down for his urination. It was funny how simple things changed just because you had lost an appendage. If they didn't sort his foot out he sure as hell wasn't going to stand like a flamenco dancer every time he wanted a piss. Sitting down, he swore at the broken lock and then stared inanely at the message imploring him to wash his hands when he had finished. He grunted. Never had he washed them after a pee. If the whole business was required then yes, but not otherwise. Even in the asylum they had never insisted on it.

Thinking back, he realized how happy he had been there. Yes, they had thought he was mad, but at least they had just wanted to feed him and help him, maybe even play some Scrabble. He used to piss off that nurse, what was her name, Calonoski? Every day she brought in the crossword and he would complete it when she wasn't looking. Drove her mad. Which was alright, as she was in an asylum.

And the drugs had been good. Some cracking highs, he remembered. Some lows too, but at least they had been able to control his dreams. Actually no, they hadn't. It was his separation from this dark world that had kept his dreams pure. Well, normal, anyway. Some of the ladies in his dreams were certainly not pure.

Standing on his remaining foot to reach the toilet roll and complete his ablutions, Austerley stopped dead as he heard the door of the museum open. There was no call, no hello, no welcome. It couldn't be Miss Goodritch. She would have said something. And she would definitely have said something when she reached my hidey-hole and found me absent. Oh, hell.

Austerley was frozen in his standing position, trousers down around his ankles. This was not a heroic moment in anyone's book. Something was fumbling outside and he heard doors open and close, then the cupboards were opened and he heard a few curses. It didn't sound like any of the pirates, but Austerley wasn't for opening the door to find out. If ever he had felt impotent, it was now. Maybe he should pull his trousers up.

The door opened. A bearded face with crusty eyes stared straight at Austerley's face. Then it scanned him up and down. Then after a "sorry governor, I'll wait" the door closed again. Pulling his trousers up quickly, Austerley opened the door and tried to grab the man's shoulder. He missed and fell sprawling across the floor.

Two hands reached under his armpits and dragged Austerley to a chair. The bearded face returned to Austerley's eyeline and looked cautiously at him.

"You're missing a foot."

The statement was so obvious it caught Austerley unaware. His usual retorts were silenced and all he could do to reply was nod. The tramp lifted Austerley's leg and examined the stump, showing no signs of embarrassment or humour.

"Did a rat get it?"

Austerley shook his head. "No, not a rat. It was a dragon."

"He's round here again. He's been causing trouble for quite a while," said the tramp knowingly. "What's your name?"

"Austerley. I'm Austerley."

"Parents mustn't have liked you. Sounds like something a Yank would say by mistake." The tramp continued his examination of Austerley's stump.

"Do you have a name?" asked Austerley.

"Yes. Yes, I do. Thanks for asking."

Austerley was dumbstruck by this response. For a man who could argue the relative merits of dimensional travel, or the intricacies of occult death rituals, these answers were just not acceptable.

"What are you doing here?"

"Looking at your foot."

"Yes, I know that."

"So why did you ask?"

"I meant what brought you in here?"

"Your foot. I thought that was obvious."

Austerley's time inside the asylum had taught him one thing. Madness can often be dealt with only by madness. You had to get inside the other person's world and stay there to communicate.

"My stump said you would come."

"It is a splendid stump. I think it probably knows more than it is letting on, governor."

"It needs your help. I think it wants you to be part of the team."

"It did tell me that."

Oh, thought Austerley, this could get complicated if my stump is talking. "I think it wants you to move it around. Did you see the wheelchair?"

"No." Austerley's shoulders dropped. "All I saw was a chariot."

Ah, thought Austerley, this is it. "Will you fetch it for me? You can be its driver."

The man nodded. This isn't going to be pleasant, thought Austerley, as he sniffed at the worsening pong emanating from the man. On fetching the chair, the man waited behind it as Austerley hauled himself up and into the seat. Comfortably seated, Austerley indicated forward, like an old coachman.

"Are you coming too?"

"Sorry?" asked Austerley.

"Are you coming too? I thought the stump wanted to go."

"It does but we're quite attached."

"Family?"

"You could say that."

This seemed to satisfy the man and he whisked the wheelchair towards the front door.

Now, thought Austerley, this is more like it. No more sulking or cowering. I'll get these ingredients myself with the man in the moon here. I'll show Kirkgordon how the real heroes do it.

The tramp opened the front door of the building and pushed the stump, and Austerley, out into the street. Looking up and down, Austerley was relieved to find that the coast was clear. He turned his head to the man pushing him.

"Do you know how to get to the DIY store?"

"Yes," said the man. Good, thought Austerley, as the tramp began to push the wheelchair up the street. He stared at the burning sky, studying the flames and the patterns on the horizon. Patterns. Yes, there were definite patterns to the picture. Flames would come and go from the same place. There were maybe fifteen seconds between the patterns, but there was definitely repetition there. No flames ever did that. And it was clever, thought Austerley, because the heat from the sky made it hard to stare at it for long. But that's not natural. Well, not supernatural natural, anyway!

"Best weather in a long while," said the tramp to the air. "Must be getting to winter though."

"Sorry, what are you on about?"

"There's no birds. And your stump said they had flown south, so it must be winter."

"Of course," said Austerley. Whatever the hell keeps him happy, he thought.

"It'll be nice tomorrow, though."

"Will it now?" said Austerley. "Did the stump say so?"

"Red sky, governor. Red sky at night, shepherd's delight.

Not always true, mind."

It's on fire, thought Austerley. It's on fire and you think it's just a weather phenomenon. This one's far gone.

They continued for a while, traversing quiet streets with the occasional onlooker staring from their windows. Sometimes people waved in desperation. The tramp, in his long black coat and brown trousers with open-toed sandals, waved back.

"People are so friendly round here, Austerley, so very friendly."

Funny, thought Austerley, most look terrified to me.

Presently the tramp turned a corner and pushed the wheelchair into a small park area. There was a little pond with some small green foliage around its edges. The tramp positioned the wheelchair beside a wooden bench and sat down. He stared at the pond and smiled. Austerley looked around, wondering why they were here, and realizing this wasn't a rest stop, he ventured to find out.

"I asked if you knew the way to the DIY store."

"Yes, you did."

"And do you?"

"Yes." The tramp nodded confidently.

"Well, this isn't the store."

"No, it's not. I'm glad you noticed. You ask a lot of questions. I was beginning to think you were a bit thick. I'm glad you're not."

"So why are we not at the store? I asked to go to the store."

"No, you didn't. You never asked that." The tramp was becoming agitated.

"I bloody well did," argued Austerley. "I asked if you knew the way to the DIY store."

"And I said yes!" shouted the tramp. "You never said you

wanted to go there. Maybe you are thick. Besides, your stump wanted some fresh air and a quiet spot."

Austerley forced himself to calm his rage. He had seen the nurses and assistants at the asylum have to deal with this sort of pedantic attitude and becoming angry never helped. Taking charge of things and becoming a hero was proving more difficult than he had anticipated. But that fire was still wrong. This was not a path to hell, so where were they?

The ageing he had undergone wasn't helping. Austerley was no fitness fanatic, but at least before losing the foot he had been able to walk about and generally get on with things. Now, after the rapid onset of years, he seemed to be all brain and no brawn. Meanwhile, he had his complement right beside him. Damn, this was pathetic. To hell with Farthington for taking his foot, to hell with Havers for using him and to hell with Churchy for shooting him in the foot in the first place.

Farthington. The name kept coming back. Havers had said the dragon had been furious at losing his pay packet from Dagon, and he blamed Austerley for it. Stupid arse, as if demons ever come through on their promises. But they did remember. And, like a demented elephant, they didn't forgive.

There was a picture forming in Austerley's mind. All the little strands of this nightmare were beginning to take shape. What if, what if? Permutations swam through Austerley's mind as he recalled old practices and chants, tales and folklore. Havers was here, Kirkgordon was here, Austerley himself was here. But Calandra was missing. Calandra, his friend and part-time protector, wasn't here. Surely she should have been factored in too? How did this all fit together, he wondered.

The tramp tapped him on the shoulder and pointed to some figures that had entered the little retreat. Two ghostly deckhands were walking towards the odd couple, each brandishing a knife and with eyes intently fixed on Austerley.

"That's him," said one of the deckhands. "The one we had at Gibbet Point, looking a bit older now. The captain wants him, alive he said, so don't go roughing him too much." The detail was good, thought Austerley, just like the records Miss Goodritch had brought out. Exactly like the drawings from the museum. But those drawings had been completed a hundred years after Captain Smith died. And yet the detail is exactly the same. Exactly.

"They want the stump," shouted Austerley. They're going to take the stump away and do it in!"

The tramp jumped up and flew into a rage. Charging at the ghosts in front of him, he leapt at them only to be swept aside by a strong arm. It had barely slowed the deckhands by a moment, but it was long enough.

Austerley was chanting under his breath, slowly and calmly. And beside him a form was rising. A tall and impressive man appeared in a bluish haze.

This is the one, thought Austerley. The stuff of legend, he laughed to himself. Who needs to move to be a hero?

A Spin Around Town

Austerley smiled evilly at the approaching deckhands. Next to Austerley stood the bluish figure, now fully materialized, in garb that was once a familiar sight in this town. The colourful, flamboyant style of the military uniform brought back memories of what had been thought of as an honourable way to fight, by all except those who had to face the barrage of muskets and swords, cannon and canister.

Austerley turned to the figure and ordered, "Sergeant, take down those brigands ahead of you. Double quick, if you please."

"With pleasure, sir," snapped the sergeant in reply before drawing a pair of muskets. He let the deckhands reach point blank range before firing and hitting them both in the chest. They tumbled backwards to the ground and disappeared into green smoke.

"You have some weird friends," said the tramp, picking himself up from the ground. "At least your stump is safe."

"Yes," agreed Austerley with a tinge of irony. "I don't know what we would do without him." He clicked his fingers and the sergeant turned back into blue gas and vanished. Oh yeah, thought Austerley, I have got the hang of this place now. I'm beginning to see how he's done this.

The tramp returned to Austerley and announced that the

stump wanted to leave. Austerley thought hard, knowing that he still needed the ingredients from the DIY store.

"Do you think I might lead the way now?" asked Austerley.

The tramp thought for a moment. "Only if it's okay with the stump."

"Well, the stump says yes and it wants to go to the DIY store."

"Excellent, it's talking to you too," said the tramp, slapping Austerley on the shoulder. And the merry team took to the streets again, Austerley's stump riding in pride of place.

It took a while to walk, and wheel, the streets of the town, and they passed mainly through residential areas. Most of the houses had the sanctuary sign on them. That's why there are so few deckhands about, thought Austerley. In fact, given the current circumstances, Austerley almost felt good about himself. The world wasn't exactly his, but it was a bit kooky and he was the one kicking it into shape. There was no better ego massage.

As they descended a hill, Austerley could see smoke in the distance. Damn. Disturbances like this were bound to bring the captain's men running. The tramp, however, seemed unperturbed.

"Is that something on fire?" asked Austerley.

"Certainly is," answered the tramp, "but it's not a problem, in fact it's going to help us."

"Why?"

"Because that's your DIY store. We certainly won't miss it now."

Oh crap, thought Austerley, that's all I need. More to the point, I need to get the man in the moon here onto a new track. "We don't want to get too close to that," he said to the tramp. "My stump never likes heat. Maybe we should get some protective cream. Let's go to the herbalist. Do you know where that is?"

"Of course. I have been in this town for the last century and four years before that. We need to go this way. But only because the stump is nodding in agreement with you." The tramp turned the wheelchair around and headed in the opposite direction. Austerley was going to complain but as he didn't know where he was going either, the blind would have to lead. He shook his head in bewilderment.

A half hour later, in a small shopping precinct on the edge of town, Austerley stared at the shop window in front of him. There were all sorts of tea pots for sale. Small dinky china pots, hand decorated with prices to match. Gaudy large pots with images of flowers that Austerley thought showed all the chromatic perception of a blind man. Cups and saucers littered the shelves inside along with a huge array of teas. Every taste was catered for in this highly specialist shop.

"I asked for the herbalist," said Austerley. "What the hell is this?"

"She sells herbal tea. Apparently it's very good for you. Especially your bowels. Makes her a herbalist. Herbal tea, made by a herbalist. That's your herbalist." The tramp looked very smug. This is too much, declared Austerley to himself. Time to change my plans.

"Do you think the stump would like a ride in a car? It would be more pleasant for him," Austerley asked the tramp. This caused a bit of commotion before an answer was forthcoming.

"What sort of car?"

"Does it matter?"

"Of course. The stump needs a classy car. Not something that would ruin his image."

I am going to lose it soon with this guy, thought Austerley. But then he spied a sports car. Not being a person to care much about them, he didn't know what type of sports car it was, but surely it would be good enough. "How about that one?" he asked.

The tramp nodded and wheeled Austerley over to it. Looking inside, Austerley saw the one thing he was hoping to find. A GPS device. The door wasn't locked and Austerley shuddered as the tramp opened the door and pulled a dead body from the car. The body was that of an older man in a smartly cut suit with a pair of expensive looking shades. Setting the body down gently, the tramp thanked the man for his car. This is just wrong, thought Austerley, but what else can I do?

The tramp helped Austerley into the passenger seat and then went around and got into the driver's seat. Austerley was going to object but the car wasn't an automatic, which ruled out Austerley from driving it.

"Do you know how to jump start this?" Austerley asked his partner, waiting for another weird response.

"Oh yes, all you need is some Meikle juice. But I thought I would use the keys instead."

Austerley had missed them hanging there. That was good, though, and he was delighted at the sound of the engine coming on. He fired up the GPS and waited for the map screen to appear. That was strange. The device said it was picking up satellites. Unless hell had gotten up to speed on the communication front, this meant Dillingham was where it should be. An illusion, it was all an illusion. These were Farthington's tactics. Then this is revenge, and most likely a fight to the death, thought Austerley. Still, I have the upper hand. He input the name of the church into the GPS.

"Okay, just listen to the woman who speaks and follow her instructions," Austerley ordered his driver. Time to regroup and see this afresh. The car, silver with streaks of black down either side, tore away from the tea shop and Austerley felt his head smack against the headrest.

The tramp brought the sun visor down and Austerley realized he was wearing the dead man's sunglasses. An incredulous look brought a defensive response from the tramp.

"He said I could have them." Seeing Austerley's surprise, he added, "What? You never heard the dead speak?"

Well, he's got me there, thought Austerley.

It had been a long time since Austerley had driven, and although he had spent a long time in America, he still remembered that here at home, cars were driven on the left-hand side. However, the tramp seemed to favour the right-hand side. Only about thirty percent of the time was the left the side of choice.

"Have you driven before?" asked Austerley.

"I used to drive Her Majesty, actually," the tramp retorted. "It's not easy with all those horses in front of you."

Austerley hung on to the handle above his head as the tramp threw the car the wrong way round a roundabout. His methods were wild, but at least he was getting nearer to their destination.

Austerley sensed something above the car that made him uncomfortable. Overtaken by a feeling of dread, he wound down the window to see what was causing it. Flying above him were the head and wings of a giant hawk with the rear of a horse hanging beneath. He quickly rolled his head back inside as the creature landed its hooves on the top of the car.

"Step on it. We've got trouble up above."

"Turn right in one hundred metres," came the soothing voice

of the GPS navigator. The tramp pitched the car round the bend, hitting kerbs on both sides of the road. Austerley bounced in his seat, clinging to his seatbelt.

"On Dancer, on Prancer, on Dunder and Blixem!" yelled the tramp.

"Your destination is on the right, five hundred metres ahead."

Austerley felt the hooves thunder against the roof of the car and then saw the bird-horse swoop low to their right-hand side. It swung back and clattered into the car, which flipped over and raced along the street on its roof. Sparks blazed from the top of the vehicle. It came to a halt some one hundred metres from the church.

Austerley unbuckled and dragged himself out of his shattered window. Glass cut into his sides and hands but he steeled himself to keep going. He heard a snort and felt hot breath on his neck. He looked up to see a giant eagle's beak, large wings and a set of hooves about to step on him. He tried to utter some summoning phrases, but he was too shaken to speak anything aloud. All he could do was wait for the impact.

An arrow hit the creature right in its belly. Unbelievably, from the core of the arrow emerged hundreds of tiny men with hammers who began to set upon the beast. It reared up and fell backwards. The face of a young girl filled Austerley's view, and he felt himself being dragged towards the church. They broke the seal of the sanctuary and the priest beside him let the girl back out into the street. In the distance the winged creature was attempting to flee but it was still covered by miniature men.

Kirkgordon was next to break the sanctuary seal, carrying the tramp on his shoulder. Kirkgordon dumped the tramp on the ground and rushed over to Austerley. He pulled Austerley's top up and plucked out some large pieces of glass. Satisfied, Kirkgordon sat on his knees beside Austerley with a look of annoyance.

"Just where the hell have you been? And who is this guy?"

"I, sir? Why, I am Father Christmas himself," declared the tramp before Nefol could take him by the hand and lead him inside.

"A relative, I take it," said Kirkgordon.

"He's just a tramp."

"And your driver. Where have you been? You were meant to be back here two hours ago. And where are Havers and Miss Goodritch?"

"Miss Goodritch was on an errand and never came back. And I think they have Havers."

"No way. Not Havers. They can't have," said Kirkgordon, with an air of desperation. "He'll be tortured to hell and back."

"Yes, by Farthington. I know he's here."

"How do you know that? Doesn't matter anyway, I bloody met him, face to face."

"Churchy, it's not what it looks like. This place is a trap. For you, for me, for Havers. All a trap. The hybrid creatures, too, I think. He's created all this just to get us. This is his vengeance. You won't believe the lengths he's gone to, or what I have seen."

"Trust me, I will. You ain't seen what I keep in my quiver!"

Dangerous Streets

Jane was feeling somewhat happier now that Wilson was protecting her. But he had taken a severe beating when the spider had tossed him aside, and the toll was starting to show. Although he easily kept up with her, his breathing was getting deeper and more laboured as he moved at a pace which she imagined wasn't close to his top speed.

The situation on the road had become more fraught, too. With the fire blazing, a large number of deckhands had come running, and Jane and her protector had to travel through back gardens and up alleyways towards the herbalist. Moving a trolley by this route took a lot of effort. When they finally reached the herbalist's street, they found their way blocked by a large congregation of ghosts.

"That may be a problem, Miss Goodritch. There's no way we will be able to get close to the shop with that many ghosts in the way. The house looks sealed as well, so we won't even be able to get inside without trapping ourselves. I take it things can be passed through the barrier?"

"I hope so," replied Jane. "We surmised that normal things would behave normally but there are different rules for people and ghosts."

"Well, given that Mr Austerley deemed it necessary to send

you out for these objects on your own, we can assume that their procurement cannot wait. I am afraid that I am going to have to leave you on your own again. And this time without a machete."

"What are you suggesting, Mr Wilson?"

"A chase, Miss Goodritch, I shall lead them all in a merry chase. I shall be the pied piper and they will follow my tune, allowing you to converse with the shopkeeper and obtain the required ingredients. Then we can rendezvous at the trolley and make for the museum. Any questions, Miss Goodritch?"

Jane was about to speak but declined. Of course this is what had to happen, and Wilson was brave in doing it. It just seemed that everything was drawing the danger ever closer, and she was losing her friends, or at least her colleagues, one at a time. Who knew if Mr Austerley was okay? Her return was well overdue. Instead she nodded her reluctant approval to Wilson and crouched in the depths of a garden to watch what was happening up ahead.

Wilson circuited the shop so that he appeared on the opposite side from the garden in which Jane was hiding. He appeared nonchalantly at the top end of the street, allowing himself to be spotted, before taking flight from the pursing group. Jane counted twelve pursuers. She waited for a minute and then approached the shop. At the window was a balding man, in his late fifties perhaps, who jumped back in surprise at her appearance. Frantically he waved at her to get away, making a charade of ghosts and pirates. She tried to calm him by waving her hand and mouthing "I know".

She slapped her list against the window and mouthed "I really need these", then indicated that he should disappear into the shop and fetch them. The man studied the list before mouthing "why?" Jane raged at him, mouthing obscenities silently to avoid attracting attention. The man, visibly shocked by her reaction, held three fingers in the air and turned back inside the shop. Watching him turn away and realizing he meant three minutes, Jane ran back to her hiding place in the garden.

Three minutes later she was back, and the bald man pushed a package out of his door and through the barrier. His hand slammed into the invisible obstruction but the package sailed through. Jane smiled her thanks and ran as quickly as she could, leaping over a fence into a garden and rounding two other corners to where the trolley was waiting. She spied a coal bunker, opened the lid and climbed inside, praying that Wilson would make his return quickly. She decided to give him a half hour and then she would make her own way back to the museum. If she was alone, she reckoned her chances were minimal.

It's like a bloody maze here, thought Wilson. By now he had lost track of exactly where he was. His ribs ached where he had collided with the racking, and he was sure his left arm was beginning to seize up. But they were close behind him, maybe only fifty metres. He cut left down a small alley then turned right into a narrow lane. Another left took him onto the cobbles and the next right would...

A ghost came round the next corner at full speed and Wilson, already committed to turning that corner, whipped his machete across the deckhand's chest, knocking him over. Fighting to keep his balance, Wilson stumbled straight into a large crab's claw. His head clattered into it and he struggled to remain upright. Back-pedalling, he could hear the shouts of his pursuers. The mass that was chasing him would be difficult to get through, but before him stood a twelve-foot bear with crab's claws emerging from its waist. There was no way to get around it in the narrow alley and Wilson made the best of two bad choices.

He charged headlong into the mass, slashing at the first deckhand and driving him into the oncoming crowd. The sheer mass of pursuers eventually pushed him back, but not before he had sliced into at least three of them with the machete. As they turned into gas, he lashed at the next two in line, felling them. His shoulder took a cutlass blow from a ghost, but he managed to keep his good arm moving, eliminating two more. His feet continued to drive and his nimbleness with the blade took out another two. Out of breath and panting heavily, he lashed wildly at the last two, clipping one, before rolling sideways to avoid the other's lunge. From the floor he threw the machete into the last deckhand and tried to get back on his feet.

Wilson screamed as an enormous claw grabbed his ankle and he was hoisted into the air and dangled in front of the face of the bear. A clawed hand smashed into his side and he swung in the air like a pendulum. Then he was swiped from the other side. As he came to rest back in front of the bear's face, Wilson could see its two huge bear arms swinging out at either side, preparing to crush him in a brutal clap. He closed his eyes and let go a prayer, knowing his time was through.

He felt a sharp pain on the inside of his left thigh. For a moment he thought he had been shot but he then realized it was a mere flesh wound. What he didn't see was the arrow, having nicked his thigh, sailing into the neck of the bear. The bear seemed stunned. A wind began to blow.

Kirkgordon stared in horror at the vortex opening up in the bear. No, no, no! Not that one! A vortex like the one he had opened in the basement began to pull everything towards it. The body of the bear was being sucked into it and the animal howled loudly.

Kirkgordon and Nefol had arrived in the electric car just in time to see Wilson finishing off the last of the ghosts, and Kirkgordon had run into the alley after him. The alley was tightly lined with backyard walls. Horrified by the bear's battering of Wilson, Kirkgordon had quickly drawn an arrow at random and fired it. Now he knew his mistake. Nefol leapt out of the car and raced to grab Wilson. From a bag at her side, she produced a small grappling iron and threw it over the wall. She held on to Wilson while battering the claw holding his ankle with her knife.

Kirkgordon felt the wind in his hair as the vortex took effect. Half the bear disappeared but the claw remained closed around Wilson's leg. Nefol's grapple was straining and looked as though it would give way at any moment. Kirkgordon inspected the contents of his quiver and made a calculation. No, he thought, I can't be sure. The grapple began to slide. Oh sod it, he thought.

Kirkgordon found an arrow with the same flashing as the previous one and fired it into the wall behind him. He heard Nefol shouting and turned to see the grapple give way. Nefol, Wilson and the claw flew towards the vortex, but Kirkgordon was unaffected. The claw disappeared up to its point and then vanished along with Wilson's shoe. Wilson himself was suspended in mid-air as the new vortex started to counteract the old one. Kirkgordon ran towards Wilson and Nefol. Reaching out, he grabbed hold of Nefol, and with his other hand he reined in her grapple.

The old vortex started to die and its pull on Wilson and Nefol began to weaken. Kirkgordon threw the grapple onto the opposite wall and felt himself and his friends being pulled towards the new vortex, the old one finally spent.

"Hang on, everyone, we're not done yet," shouted Kirkgordon over the raging wind. Nefol holding Wilson with one hand and with an arm around Kirkgordon, Kirkgordon with the grapple rope wrapped around his arm, the company moved through the air, watching some debris that had escaped the first vortex fly past their heads. Gradually the wind relented. They fell to the floor and Kirkgordon felt the burns from the rope on his arm.

"Is he okay?" asked Kirkgordon, seeing Nefol tend to Wilson.

"I think so. He looks pretty banged up. He needs my father's help, I think. Let's get him to the car."

Wilson started to gesticulate with his hands. "G... Good... Herb..."

"What's he saying?" asked Kirkgordon.

"Gibberish. Let's get him to my father before it's too late."

"No, Nefol, wait. Listen, he's trying to say something."

"Herb... herbalist... Goodritch... help... herbalist..."

"He said Goodritch. He means Jane. Austerley said she was going to the herbalist. Is there one round here?" Nefol nodded. Kirkgordon picked Wilson up and carried him back to the car. He laid him across the back seat as comfortably as he could, but his legs had to be squashed up.

"Okay, Nefol, we go to the herbalist and see if Miss Goodritch is anywhere around. Pick her up and get back to the church as quickly as possible. Okay?"

Nefol nodded but looked sternly at Kirkgordon.

"What? What's the matter? Did I leave something out?"

Nefol shook her head but uttered two words. "No arrows!"

Debate

Everyone was back in sanctuary at the church. Well, not everyone, thought Kirkgordon. Havers was somewhere, maybe in a box, maybe imprisoned or running riot, but certainly not here and not in touch. There was now a man called Wilson on the scene. One of Havers' government men, apparently, and he looked like him too. Mannerisms, speech and gait, all befitting of Havers. But I'll be taking the lead, Mr Wilson. Well, I am an employee too and it's time we got a proper handle on what is going on.

The lounge of the church manse was the venue for what Kirkgordon hoped would be an enlightening exchange of knowledge. Father Jonah was sat in the largest chair of the room. Rather than dethrone him, Kirkgordon chose to stand, giving him the air of a detective summing up at the end of a novel. Austerley had a chair, as did Miss Goodritch. Wilson sat on a stool while Nefol sat cross-legged on the floor.

"Alright, everyone," said Kirkgordon. "I thought it best to pull together for a moment and work out what's happening and what we are going to do about it. There are two main issues. One, where is Havers? Is he alive, dead, trapped or whatever else gets thrown up in our line of work? Two, what's happening in Dillingham and how do we stop it?"

"I can answer that one for you," grunted Austerley.

"No, Indy, in a moment. First we have to introduce a new member of our illustrious band of heroes. Wilson, I think you need to tell us all who you are and why you are here."

Austerley folded his arms and sulked.

"Certainly, Mr Kirkgordon, certainly," smiled Wilson, "Like many of you, I work for SETAA."

"Who's SETAA?" asked Miss Goodritch.

"Major Havers never said?" replied Wilson. "Well, it stands for Supernatural and Elder Threat Assessment Agency, and we are the unknown agency that deals with... well, the sort of thing that's out there, really. Spiders with bird's legs, and all that."

"How do we know you're SETAA?" Austerley pitched in.

"Indy, will you give him a minute?" Kirkgordon rolled his eyes.

"Well, Farthington wasn't. He was bloody well just like Havers, Churchy. Just like him, and look what happened because of him. Lost my foot, in case you hadn't noticed."

"Indy, all the blind people in the world couldn't fail to know you have lost your foot! And it's good to know Farthington's now to blame and not me. Just shut up a minute and let the man speak."

Austerley snorted in disgust.

"It is a valid point, Mr Kirkgordon," Wilson said smoothly. Austerley pulled a face. "I was sent here by Major Havers before any of you. The priest knows that." Father Jonah nodded. "Father Jonah had suspicions about what was going on in the town. High levels of occult activity."

"Yes," interrupted the priest, "and I didn't need any instruments either. You could feel it, the evil. I said to Havers there was vengeance brewing. Someone was being twisted in the devil's hands, nature was being abused. I called it in but Havers didn't take me seriously and sent this young lad instead. Not your fault, son."

"Thank you, Father. My mission was to observe only. I could see there was something happening at the care home but it took several weeks to spot the markers being left beside residents' beds."

"Like the brooch I saw beside Austerley," said Kirkgordon. "I brought one back from the home." He threw it to Wilson.

"That's it. When these markers were left, the residents would age thirty years in a matter of days and end up looking, well, no offence, like Mr Austerley here. I followed the care staff one night and ran into a ghostly apparition that took several hacks at me, leaving me incapacitated. They brought me back to the care home and dumped me in one of the large commercial bins at the back of the building. I was tied and gagged but I managed to escape. I don't know how long I was there but the sky was on fire when I climbed out. Running through the town, I saw a mark on all the houses and people trapped inside.

"My first idea was that I should get to the church, but the whole area had a ghostly horde around it. I couldn't inflict any damage on them, I knew that from my first scrape. So I went further out of town and found that the DIY shop hadn't been sealed. I managed to break in and get some food but then I was joined by a horrible creature that was a spider crossed with a bird. I decided to rest up in the office where the beast couldn't enter and watch on the security monitors for anyone coming in. That's when I met Miss Goodritch on her shopping trip."

"She was getting items for me in order to deal with this problem," Austerley chipped in.

"How did Havers know you were in trouble?" asked the priest.

"This new crew got here very quickly after your disappearance. I doubt Havers would have been worried by you being missing for a few days."

"Internal alarm. Had one in my jacket and pressed it during that first attack. It's only pressed when you think you have been compromised to a point where you believe you will die." For a moment the room was silent.

Austerley spoke first. "Why don't I have one?"

"That would seem obvious to me," came Kirkgordon's automatic retort.

"He said you two were like this," observed Wilson. "Major Havers told us all not to be worried about his judgement. They're not like us, he said. But he told us that you had certain skills. He said you were dogged, Mr Kirkgordon. Like a dog on its chewy toy, you would work it over and over until it gave in. And you, Mr Austerley, he said you were the most dangerous genius that he had ever known."

Austerley smiled and sat up slightly, milking the silent applause. "Anything else about me?"

"Yes," answered Wilson. "We were told that if you went south that elimination was to be considered with extreme prejudice."

Austerley gulped. "Anything more?"

"Just a personal opinion. We don't normally give those in briefings but he was insistent."

"Something flattering, no doubt," said Austerley.

"No," Wilson said flatly. "He said he thought you to be a total arse."

Kirkgordon burst out laughing. Austerley refolded his arms with another almighty grunt that contained some swearing.

Kirkgordon recovered himself and turned to Austerley. "See

if you can leave the arse aside and give us some of that genius to tell us what is happening round here."

"Forgive me if I don't stand," said Austerley, "but it's a long story about a supposed friend."

Kirkgordon chuckled internally. Damn, he's rattled, he thought.

Austerley continued. "There is something very amiss with what is happening and I believe that the priest was correct in his original assumption."

"You mean someone is in league with the devil?" asked Miss Goodritch.

"Well, that is a question that requires clarification, Miss Goodritch," Austerley replied. "After all, we are all at times in league with the devil by our actions, are we not, Father?" Father Jonah gave a simple nod. "That being said, I believe there is witchcraft afoot, but it is not being used in the way we believe it to be. The impression given was that Dillingham had been plucked and taken on an interdimensional ride to hell. This is a falsehood. I was able to receive a GPS signal in the car."

"The one you totalled?" asked Nefol.

Austerley glared at her. "Yes. The sports car. The one wrecked by the winged creature." He took a deep breath. "Dillingham has not moved. I was tricked into believing that I had stopped its motion, but that motion was never interdimensional. It was only ever a minor induced quake."

"Never having been on one of those, it did fool me," noted Miss Goodritch.

"But how did you miss it, Indy?" asked Kirkgordon. "Pride?"

"I admit, Churchy, that I was somewhat overcome at my success, but to be fair, which no one seems to be any more, I had been drugged to the hilt and I was standing next to a ghost with a naked woman dancing close by. And we can all be taken in by these naked dancing women."

Touché, thought Kirkgordon, touché.

"It occurred to me, while we were operating in this limbo, waiting for Dillingham to descend further to hell, to wonder why hadn't it happened earlier," continued Austerley. "There were plenty of bodies to draw power from in the hospital. Our descent should have continued quickly. But that wasn't the game. Similarly for the ghosts, the deckhands and Captain Smith. Nasty in one sense, but not really the hounds of hell. And none of them were surprised at today's modern technology."

Kirkgordon was puzzled. "I'm not with you, Indy."

Austerley tutted. "A soul or being from the past would be stunned at today's wonders. A car would take them aback. They would be amazed by them. But something conjured from the mind of a modern person? That creature would be at home with the present, like its master. Or mistress, in this case."

"Tania! You think Tania's controlling the ghosts, not resurrecting a spirit?" blurted Kirkgordon. "Previously, you said she'd been infused with a dead witch's spirit."

"Oh, she's a witch alright, one of the continued line of Dillingham witches, as I found out from Miss Goodritch's records. But one who has been schooled in subterfuge. I'm amazed Havers didn't see it."

"Dammit, Indy, just say it straight."

"I thought he did, Mr Kirkgordon," interrupted Wilson. "Major Havers did say you were a little slow."

Austerley smiled and wallowed in having the room at his command and Kirkgordon cut down to size.

"Your Tania," Austerley pronounced, "is a witch, and of quite a standard too. But she's being played by Farthington."

"Zmey Gorynych?" said a stunned Wilson.

"Who's Zemmy Gorynitch?" said a bemused Miss Goodritch.

"Okay, from the top then," a proud Austerley continued. "Zmey Gorynych is a three-headed dragon, known as Farthington in his human form, and he's also the bastard that ripped my foot off."

"Always the foot," moaned Kirkgordon.

"Yes, my foot. I can't walk. I need a babysitter. I've been wheeled about by Brown Owl over there!" Austerley pointed to Miss Goodritch. "I faced up to a demon and what did I get? Nightmares and a missing foot. So forgive me, Churchy, if I am somewhat pissed off at the world at the moment. But I am missing my foot." Tears welled up in Austerley's eyes. "It might be a flaming joke to you but I am a cripple. I can't even get to the shops without crutches. I can't be hauled around by the collar anymore like you used to, dragging my butt out of trouble. Now I'm dependant on someone actually carrying me. Shit, Churchy, I want my foot back!"

"Mind your language in front of the child!" ordered Wilson.

"Shove it up your jacksie, newbie. It's your kind that got me into this crappy state." Austerley buried his head in his hands and started to weep bitterly. Father Jonah stood and walked across the silent room, put his arms around Austerley and just held him.

Well, thought Kirkgordon, that didn't go as planned. "Let's take a few moments," he suggested, and he started to wave everyone out of the room. In a few moments, Kirkgordon was left standing looking at Austerley cradled like a baby in the priest's arms. His crying continued, accompanied by great sniffs. During the whole time, Father Jonah said nothing.

"Sorry, Indy," muttered Kirkgordon. "I'm sorry I ever let you go to that graveyard up at Gainsborough. I'm sorry you ever came out of the asylum. I'm just sorry. You didn't deserve to lose the foot. I'm sorry."

"I know," Austerley mumbled. "You shouldn't have had to try and kill me. It was my fault. All of it. I know my curiosity, the trouble it causes. But I love it, the mystery, the power. Dammit, Churchy, it's how I'm made."

"Yeah, I know."

"But it's my foot!"

Kirkgordon watched Austerley double over in tears again. He felt hollow inside. He felt responsible. Always trying to save everyone, that's what Alana had said.

"You're not the only one with a curse," Kirkgordon mumbled quietly at Austerley as he left the room.

Manhunt

He nearly lashed out. The reflex almost kicked in but something within stopped it. An inner voice screamed at him that he wasn't under attack, that the bony hand which grabbed his wrist was doing so out of desperation, not malevolence.

"They took your friend. Took him away, didn't they? He had the brooch by his bed. Is he older now? Has he aged? I used to have looks before they took them. Used to have a body that worked. It's all breaking down. Everything is stopping, son."

Kirkgordon realized it was Mrs Moor, the woman Tania had claimed to be unsound in mind. Her wrists felt like sheer bone. Once his eyes had adjusted to the dark, he wished they had stayed blind. The woman's face was taut across her skull, eye sockets set deep. She didn't look ill. She looked drained. Drained of life.

"It's too late, son. I'm just moving on," she said in a hoarse whisper. "I'll see my Jack soon. That'll be good. Jack's waited fifty years for me. Will see him soon, I guess. That's good." Her head fell into Kirkgordon's lap. He sat and stroked her hair gently, and her breathing became more laboured. Each breath drew out longer than the last. After five long minutes, she ceased her struggle.

At least she's out of here, clear of it all, thought Kirkgordon.

Then the dilemma struck him. He knew what the right thing to do would be but he wanted to carry out the other option. She should be buried. With dignity and respect. Her life noted. Instead, he knew he would leave her body here, and then, who knows? Well, yes, who did know? Why this? You're sat up in that heaven and You give me this. Why did she die like this? I know there's evil here but You tell me You are stronger. So why, God, why? Why this suffering? Why am I left to stop it?

Kirkgordon realized he didn't have time for these thoughts. In reality, he had fifteen minutes now to get in, grab whatever he needed – even though he didn't know what that was – and then get out and rescue Graham. This wasn't looking good. But there was no point thinking about it now. It was time to act. Hopefully he wouldn't have to pay for his ten minutes of compassion.

There was another door out of the boiler house leading to the main building. Kirkgordon pressed his ear to it and listened attentively. There was no sound on the other side so he gently opened the door. Given the position of the boiler house, he knew he needed to make a left towards the residents' rooms. Everything was silent. It was unnerving not to hear the occasional patient wandering about or babbling out loud. Even the quiet conversations and the momentary banter of staff and patients were absent. Last time, the fresh smell of disinfectant had wafted down the corridors but now even that sensual invasion was lacking.

Proceeding slowly and carefully, Kirkgordon checked each room he passed that had an open door. It took him four rooms to find an occupant, an elderly woman sleeping in her bed beneath a floral patterned quilt. He noted her peaceful breathing. She was probably drugged. On the cabinet beside her bed was a small emerald brooch. One item recovered, thought Kirkgordon as he pocketed it.

He was about to exit the room when he heard a wicked laugh. He stretched himself against the inner wall and held his breath. A ghostly green figure walked past the room, oblivious to his presence. Stepping out, Kirkgordon noticed the door in the middle of the complex. It had the sign "Staff Only" emblazoned upon it and a heavy lock. Worth a look, he thought, and he checked the surrounding corridors to make sure he was alone. About a thirty second job to open this, he reckoned.

Taking a small screwdriver from his new trousers, Kirkgordon worked coolly and methodically, always listening to the sounds of the care home. After careful work and a few deft touches, the lock opened and Kirkgordon slipped quietly inside.

There was a small flight of stairs which led down to a dark room. Open shelving with many cardboard boxes of nursing supplies filled the area, looking like a makeshift supermarket. Kirkgordon trod gently, checking every aisle. Delving into the occasional box, only sanitary products and basic healthcare items came to hand: large incontinence pads, lotions, bathing sponges, bed pans, bandages, tape. Nothing untoward.

But something wasn't quite right. The orientation of the racking looked a little strange. In the far right corner, there was some missing, as if someone hadn't measured up correctly. There was a space from one rack to the other the width of a person. Also, the opposite end had a particularly crushed look to it and Kirkgordon wondered why the space hadn't been utilized to relieve the crush.

He approached the exposed wall, intending to check its authenticity by sounding it out with his fist. He raised his hand

and went to rap the wall gently. But his fist went clean into the wall. There was no resistance and the fist disappeared. He could still feel his wrist and hand but where it should have been, there was just a wall. Kirkgordon took a random item from his person, one of his lock picks. Kneeling down, he reached through the wall and set down the item. Then he withdrew his hand before placing it back through the wall to retrieve the lock pick. Satisfied, he stepped through the wall.

An illusion, Kirkgordon decided, before his surroundings took his breath away. He had walked into a miniature zoo. The cramped room contained cages of glass and metal arranged in narrow aisles, similar to the racks of care products in the previous room. Spiders and cockroaches, snakes and birds, even lobsters and fish: an array of wildlife was scattered about. Looking into some of the cages, Kirkgordon was taken aback. He remembered the winged snake that had exploded when pierced by his arrow. Many of the cages contained such mutations, but in a much smaller form. The abhorrent nature of the hybrid creatures took him aback but there was something else bothering Kirkgordon. Having reached the end of the first aisle, he was convinced someone was behind him.

Grabbing an arrow, Kirkgordon turned and drew his bow. He struggled to hold his aim at the target's head.

"Now, now, Churchy, feel free to have a good look. After all, it was what you wanted. You're not telling me you didn't want to take this flesh of mine?" Stood opposite was Tania, fully naked and tossing her head to one side, allowing her hair to swing round from behind her shoulder.

Oh damn, thought Kirkgordon. Her body was that of a young woman, free from blemish and pert in form. He fought the arousal, reminding himself of the situation he was in, of the warnings his friends had given. But part of him was enjoying the moment, while another part struggled to remain aloof. Oh damn. Her hips were good in jeans, but unveiled... oh damn.

More by habit than decision, his bow remained drawn. Somewhere in the recesses of his mind, Kirkgordon remembered that if he fired, he had no idea what the arrow would do. Trying to focus elsewhere, he brought Alana to mind, visualizing her in all her glory. The picture was exquisite and tapped his deepest urges.

"But she doesn't accept you, does she?"

His throat went dry.

"Oh, I know you. Every bit of you. I know your desires, your longings. How she doesn't like your new friends, how she hates your job. She doesn't understand your importance, and you won't tell her lest you frighten her away. Well, I don't frighten. And this... this is how you like your women, is it not?"

Kirkgordon swallowed hard while taking in the view. There wasn't a single blemish on her perfect skin. She seemed to be ideal in her proportions, and her forwardness and sheer nakedness set his inner wildness alight. But she was also poison, dangerous, playing on his relationship with Alana. Sweat broke out on his forehead. It dripped down into his eyes, stinging them. He became aware that he was shaking slightly, trembling at the anticipation of what would happen next. His stomach felt hollow. Part of him longed for the temptation to become true, to fulfil his desire to dominate this nymph standing in front of him. Deep inside his mind a voice said no, not worth the risk. But that voice seemed distant, calling from the depths of a chasm.

Gradually, Tania turned around, letting him feast his eyes on her in full. Having hooked her worm, she began to walk slowly towards Kirkgordon, her hips swaying hypnotically, begging to be grabbed. Paralysed by this spell of flesh, Kirkgordon held his bow upright, still drawn. She moved up against his body, letting his back feel the press of her breasts. One hand snaked around him before descending between his legs. Kirkgordon started and involuntarily his hand holding the bow in tension let go.

The arrow raced from the bow and flew at pace off to the right, hitting the wall. Kirkgordon heard the words "Succumb to my touch, have me!" before all sounds were overpowered by a wind that appeared from nowhere. Kirkgordon focused his archer's eye on the spot where his arrow had landed. The wall became blurry and started to swirl. The cages in the room began to move towards where the arrow had landed and Kirkgordon felt Tania's grip change from one of seduction to one of panic. Clinging to his body, she struggled to maintain a hold. Her feet whipped round in front of Kirkgordon. Cages began to crash past them, cracking open, and the animals fought to move away from the sucking void.

But Kirkgordon felt no pressure, no drawing force from the hole that was opening. He saw cages fly into the aperture and vanish, gone from sight in an instant. Then he felt something crash into his back and both he and Tania toppled forward to the ground. She was pulled instantly towards the hole. Some racking had blocked it and was bending and straining from the inward pressure. Her naked body crashed into the racking and was left pressed against it with her legs and arms being pulled towards the void.

"Help me!" Tania screamed. "Help me, Churchy. Help me, my love!"

Just let her go. Let her go. She's brought us halfway to hell and this will put her to bed. It was Havers' voice in his head, with an echo from Austerley. It was the wise course of action, the correct decision for the betterment of humanity. But she's a person. Broken, yes, but still a person. You're not like Havers. This was Father Jonah's voice. And Alana was echoing it. She would reach out; she would always try to redeem him. And then yet another voice. She'll be thankful, she'll be beholden to you. A woman who'll lay herself at your whim. Look at that body. Kirkgordon's mind raced with all these thoughts as the racking bent further and Tania's back slid off the metal. A flailing hand saved her and she swung from the remaining racking, feet dangling into the void.

He knew there was no decision, he had only one option. People with a conscience have to enact the noble course, not the correct one. Putting his bow across him, he reached out with both hands, grabbing Tania by the wrists. Her body was thumped by the racking as it broke and disappeared into the void. Cages flew past his head, animals consigned to whatever oblivion lay beyond. His arms screamed at the pain of her nails digging into his wrists as she put all her effort into escaping the blackness behind her.

Eventually, the void began to close and Tania fell to the floor. Kirkgordon stood for a moment looking at her naked form, part of him wanting to grab and comfort her, and then to love her. Another part told him it was a lie and she wanted to destroy what he was, wanted him only as a body for her pirate. When faced with such decisions, there is only one reaction for a man. As Tania turned her head up to view her saviour, she saw his heels disappearing through the secret door. And she laughed. A cackling, wild laugh, full of glee, lust and victory.

"Mine! You'll be mine, Churchy!"

Only a Foot

Okay, huddle up everyone, it's time to make a plan." Kirkgordon had reconvened his meeting in the lounge and this time he was determined to leave with a plan of action. "Austerley, lay down the situation for us as you see it. Everyone else shut up. We need to get moving soon, so we can't be doing with interruptions." Austerley nodded and Kirkgordon's stare swept around the room to declare that any disobedience would be swiftly dealt with.

"Right then. Sorry for earlier," said Austerley. "As I said before, this is all subterfuge. Dillingham is still where it always has been. The GPS signal told me so. The fire in the sky is an illusion. Something is protecting the town from the outside world, but I don't know what. If there were no shield or blockage then Havers' people would be here by now.

"The ghosts are not an illusion but neither are they spirits of the dead. Rather, they have been summoned by someone, namely Tania, the care home worker, who is also a witch. She comes from a long line of witches, according to Miss Goodritch's museum records, and is very powerful, especially for one so young. However, I understand her magic now and there are several defences I can use against it.

"I realized her deception when I saw the drawings at the

museum. The ghosts, including Captain Smith, look exactly like those drawings, but they weren't created until two hundred years after the event. There should be differences between the drawings and the real thing, but there aren't any differences with our ghosts. Also, they show no surprise at modern technology, none at all. Therefore, they must have been conjured from a modern mind. The creatures are another matter. They seem to have been created by fusing different animals together. They are real and can be struck without requiring spiritual weapons."

"They are Tania's creations as well," interrupted Kirkgordon. "I saw her little zoo at the care home. It's destroyed now. There was a tiny accident with an arrow causing a vortex."

"You let go a vortex arrow in a confined space? Are you mad? The instruction manual specifically says not to," said Father Jonah, jumping to his feet.

"What instruction manual?" asked Kirkgordon.

"I told you to look inside the quiver. It's all there, everything you needed for your bow." Father Jonah was indignant.

"Where?" Kirkgordon was bemused.

The priest walked over to Kirkgordon's quiver and pulled out a small piece of paper stuck on the inside.

"That's it? Those are my instructions? No disrespect to you, Father, but that is totally inadequate."

The priest shook the paper in his hand and before everyone's eyes it swelled into a manual of at least a hundred pages. Handing the book to Kirkgordon, the priest sat down, his face thunderous.

"I'll continue then," said Austerley. "I believe Farthington engaged Tania's services in order to lure Havers, Kirkgordon and myself here. His intention was to bring our colleague

Calandra here too but he miscalculated, and with things already in motion, he ran with what he had. He also didn't appreciate Father Jonah's powers. The sanctuary meant that we were safe from him. Since then, he has been waiting for our move. He has Havers and I suspect he will call our bluff. I think he will flaunt Havers in front of us and declare that he will kill him unless we come forward."

"Then you can stay here and I will go," said Wilson.

"He's banking on Churchy there charging to the rescue. Unlike Havers, Kirkgordon will never leave someone behind," said Austerley.

"He's right, Wilson," said Kirkgordon. "Havers may kill me himself for it but we will rescue him. But not before Indy here levels the playing field. Showtime, Indy. Let's see what you've got from Miss Goodritch's shopping trip."

Austerley stood up on his good leg and Kirkgordon moved in beside him to act as a crutch. At Austerley's instruction, Miss Goodritch brought in a bowl, some pots, some cups and a small table. Nefol brought in the items Miss Goodritch had collected and placed them on the table.

"I am going to do three things now," said Austerley. "Number one, I will ascertain what is causing the shielding of Dillingham and whether we can destroy it. Two, I will try to find Havers. And three, I will eliminate all the ghosts and Captain Smith."

When he's not in a trance, drugged or in a bad mood, he's devastatingly good at what he does, thought Kirkgordon. Which is just as well, because without Havers, I really need pointing in the right direction.

Austerley began mixing items. At a further request, Nefol brought in a small gas burner, and the assembled gathering watched Austerley boil and mix his way through many colourful liquids. The smells emitted by the vessels were mostly repulsive, but there was one that smelt like strawberries. Soon, Austerley glanced up at his watchers to indicate that he was ready.

Pouring one mixture into the bowl, he chanted words that made no sense to Kirkgordon and that drew a shaking head from Father Jonah. Undeterred, Austerley drew his hands back and forward across the bowl.

"There's nothing evil in these chants, Miss Goodritch. I am merely drawing the energy from around us to channel it," Austerley explained.

"And you know not what you draw it from. Do not fool yourself, Mr Austerley," warned the priest. Austerley rolled his eyes and continued chanting. In the bowl, a view of the sea was materializing. Kirkgordon could see a post with a cage swinging from it.

"That's Gibbet Point," exclaimed Miss Goodritch.

"Yes," said Austerley, "and that's his device. It's a mystical generator. I can't attack it from here but it looks unprotected, merely hidden by its very normality. I venture that's not the post that was there last year."

"There was no post last year," said Miss Goodritch. "The council put that up a few months ago."

"Then it needs to be taken down," stated Kirkgordon. "Good. Right, Austerley, find Havers."

Austerley returned to mixing his ingredients. Wilson, still weak from his beating from the bear, took a seat. Austerley created several more mixtures, poured them into the bowl and stirred the water. The bowl produced a view of the care home. Austerley mumbled some more words and the picture zoomed down several corridors before arriving in front of a bed. The picture was a close up of Havers' face. It was pale and going grey. He seemed to be resting in peace.

"Is he dead?" asked Kirkgordon.

"No. If he was I wouldn't be able to find him."

"Stop," shouted the priest, "There's something else!"

Before anyone could move, a dragon's head appeared in the water. It burst out of the bowl on an elongated neck and searched wildly around the room. Finding Austerley, it fixed its gaze on him.

"Austerley, time to die!" The dragon's head drew back as it took in a breath and emitted a stream of fire at Austerley. A stunned Austerley was transfixed as the fire raged towards him. Suddenly it stopped, right in front of his face, and disappeared in an instant. Looking to the bowl, Austerley saw it had been upturned. It rested on the table with the priest's hand over it.

"I wish you wouldn't mess with these forces," said Father Jonah sternly.

After a moment's silence, Kirkgordon spoke up. "So he's in the care home. Time to undo Tania's mischief."

"Don't destroy her," urged the priest. "Make sure there is time for redemption, Mr Austerley. We all need redemption."

Austerley glowered at the priest and looked at Kirkgordon, who nodded and turned to Nefol, asking her to accompany him. Together they walked down the hall of the house to a bedroom. Nefol spoke a few words and opened the door. Lying on the bed inside, with her hands tied behind her back and her ankles tied together, was Tania. Her mouth was gagged with tape. She looked directly at Kirkgordon as he entered.

"I'm going to take the tape off," said Kirkgordon. "Listen, if I hear you say anything, any chants or words other than to speak in reply to my answers, I will knock you out again and you will be gagged. Then Austerley will have to reach inside your brain for the answers. It's not pleasant because he's not that good at it. Understand me?"

Tania nodded. She was wrapped in a sheet but her curves were still evident. Kirkgordon tried to focus on the task in hand, but her body was so distracting. At times, he wished he was blind to these womanly charms that drew him in so easily. Nefol was a good foil to his reactions, though. He thought having a youngster in the room was a stronger deterrent than his own mother. He ripped the tape off Tania's mouth.

"I see you still like to look," mocked Tania. "Ditch the kid and you can still have me!"

Kirkgordon struck her with the back of his hand. "Enough. You are a witch. A highly sexual one, but still a witch. You only want to take from me, not to give. I have a woman and you are not her." It was like a mantra, Kirkgordon thought, and despite having made it up on the spot, he thought it was pretty good. But there was safety in numbers.

He swept an arm under her, picking her up. Halfway through the manoeuvre, she parted her legs, trying to trap him, but he was wise to it. Without showing any emotion, he nodded towards the door. Nefol opened it and Kirkgordon carried Tania to the front room.

Placing her in the centre of the room, Kirkgordon withdrew to the edge. He was somewhat compromised in the matter of Tania and he didn't trust himself. Austerley, now returned to the couch, went down on his knees and crept up on Tania.

"You look old. Very old." Tania laughed, drawing a scowl from Austerley.

"Steeped in it, aren't you?" Austerley said. "Steeped. Well,

I know how you do it. I know it came from your grandmother who taught you how to gain your powers. It's all written down. Joined the coven, did you? Was your father's life worth the prize?"

"Dear God!" exclaimed Miss Goodritch.

Father Jonah closed his eyes, his lips giving up a silent prayer.

"Well, now we'll end it." Austerley laid his hands upon Tania. The witch shook violently as Austerley spoke words no one understood. The room began to shake, and green gas rushed into the room and into Tania's eyes, ears, nostrils. She screamed as the gas poured into her mouth, making her choke and spit.

As the gas continued to return, Austerley began to change. His skin became less wrinkled, and he felt his body regaining its mid-life vigour, his joints freeing.

"It is done," cried Father Jonah. "It is done."

Tania was coughing uncontrollably now and Father Jonah took her in his arms, cradling her. "Peace, child, peace. It has been put right. He has put back all you have done wrong. Relax now, be at peace. Ask and you shall receive forgiveness. You can start again, throw off your past. You have a second chance, Tania. He whom you called an enemy is now your friend. He will make you whole."

Tania began to cry, pouring out her tiredness and hurt. She looked into the priest's eyes, asking if it was true. Father Jonah nodded and began to smile. But then Tania's mouth let go an ear-piercing scream.

"No!" yelled the priest. "No!"

"An eye for an eye, is it not, Father?" shouted Austerley.

Kirkgordon was confused until he saw Tania's foot. Her toes were shrinking. One by one they were disappearing into thin air. Meanwhile, Austerley's stump was growing. The joint was renewing and a foot was beginning to grow.

Kirkgordon raced to Austerley and tried to pull him away from Tania. Austerley's face was wild and his skin red with pumping blood. A strength not born from human flesh held Austerley to Tania's body and she continued to scream.

"Yes, yes. Feel my pain!" yelled Austerley.

Miss Goodritch had joined Kirkgordon in pulling at Austerley's arm but nothing could move him. Father Jonah laid a hand on Kirkgordon and cried out for intervention, for one who was good to interrupt this madness. Kirkgordon felt a power surge in his arms and he ripped away Austerley's grip, throwing him onto the sofa.

The room fell silent except for Tania's tears. Father Jonah stood up and walked calmly over to Austerley. Austerley's face was streaked with tears and he looked like a broken man.

"I told you," Father Jonah said, pointing at Austerley. "Don't mess with these things. But you don't listen, you indulge. And now that foot shall be a curse to you, worse than when it was missing. You have passed on your pain instead of sharing it to be healed. This is anger, this is rage, this is domination and wrath. And you may have destroyed her, but you will also destroy yourself!"

Consequences

Kirkgordon breathed deeply. This was all getting too fraught for him. For someone who had limited understanding of the occult, of all this weirdness, he felt ill-equipped to be leading the charge to rescue Havers. Knowing that Havers would not permit a rescue if the circumstances were reversed, would choose instead just to let Kirkgordon go, wasn't great encouragement either. But then again, wasn't that the point? Havers was wrong in his professional view. The individual did matter, they mattered a lot.

And then there was Austerley. Just when you thought he had turned a corner, grumbling but on message, he goes and does all this. Bloody hell. The priest had been doing well with Tania, in fact she might even have been ready to accept redemption. But now?

In his time working protection, Kirkgordon had seen many a bloody sight. Bits blown off people, limbs lost, shots taken, but nothing was like watching someone's foot disappearing. Left with nothing but a bloody stump, Tania had gone wild, calling out all sorts of blasphemies. Kirkgordon had been forced to use his nerve pinch to silence her. And as for Austerley... You would have thought he would be happy, with a spring to his step, but no. He hadn't banked on Tania's foot being smaller. With a size twelve on one foot and a size three on the other, he was limping badly, constantly tilted to one side. Another three weeks and he would have had a prosthetic. Stupid arse.

Father Jonah appeared at his side. In his hands were two cups of coffee, one black and steaming, the other extremely milky.

"I thought you weren't into coffee," said Kirkgordon.

"I'm not. But you looked like you needed one and a bit of company."

"Cheers. Did I do the right thing in there?"

"Don't dwell on it. You can't second guess with people. Austerley made his own decision, which he was going to do whatever you decided. He ruined himself, Mr Kirkgordon. We can't save everyone. In fact, we can save no one."

"Tania's a gorgeous girl. Truly stunning."

"On the outside, yes. But she's black inside. You don't play with the darkness and remain untouched. Ask Mr Austerley. Or Major Havers."

"What do you mean?"

"Clinical, cold, exacting. No trust in people, just a desire for outcomes. I still hold out hope there, though."

"Your daughter was a great help, she's very resourceful. She acts older than her years."

"Yes, indeed, but then again that's Major Havers' doing." Kirkgordon threw a questioning glance but the priest refused to bite. "Be careful when you engage Farthington. Austerley will look to kill, for there's as much anger in him as there is in the dragon. Take care of your people. Remember, have a little faith. You are where you are needed. And read the arrows' instructions! Some of them are pretty deadly."

Kirkgordon laughed. "I prefer the normal sort, but they have been pretty handy. Tell me, though. You're a priest, you've seen this stuff we're pitched into. How do you find the white and not the black? How do you know what's right?"

Father Jonah thought for a moment. "Do what builds up. Do what redeems, what keeps others from hurting and destroying. Even when it's messy, even when it costs. It's what Alana will understand. It's why she's still committed."

Kirkgordon was stunned. "When did you meet my wife?"

"I haven't. Enjoy your coffee."

Kirkgordon took five minutes to drink his coffee then turned his attentions to his team members. Wilson, although mobile, was seriously hurt. He could walk, possibly jog, but he wouldn't last long in a fight. Despite much protestation, Kirkgordon decided Wilson should accompany Miss Goodritch rather than face Farthington at the care home.

"Remember," Kirkgordon told Wilson and Miss Goodritch, "we need that device causing the shield down as soon as possible. They don't know we know about it, so stay covert, Wilson, and then bring it down. There should be help ready just outside the shield." They had decided on the sewers as the preferred route, and Miss Goodritch seemed keen to help.

"Mr Wilson saved my life. Major Havers may have done too. It's my duty, Mr Kirkgordon. My duty."

"It'll be fine, Miss Goodritch. Listen to Wilson and stay safe." Kirkgordon smiled at her as she descended into the sewers, but his heart was heavy. With the ghosts gone, there were only the hybrid creatures left between Farthington and justice. But Farthington never fully trusted anything. There had to be a back-up.

Kirkgordon turned back to the manse, leaving the priest to let his smaller party out of the sanctuary. As he brooded on

Farthington's possible reinforcements, Nefol came running up.

"She's gone."

"Who?" asked Kirkgordon.

"The witch! Tania. Just gone."

"But you were watching her."

"I was, and she just vanished, right into the bed. I searched the room but there's nothing."

"Okay, get Austerley and then your father. Let's work out what's happening."

Kirkgordon ran to the bedroom that had been holding Tania. On the bedclothes lay the gown that had been covering Tania's nakedness. There were a few specks of blood at the indentation where her foot should have been. This didn't surprise Kirkgordon, but there was also a mix of blood and spit beside where her head would have been lying.

Austerley hobbled into the room. "How did the girl let her get away? That witch will have it in for me."

"Dammit, Austerley, give my head some peace. You angered her, so just shut it. I need to think."

"Peace? Peace? It's okay for you! She just wants to get her kit off for you and romp the night away. She'll be after my blood."

"And whose fault is that?"

Father Jonah entered the room. "So she chose the darkness. See the hornet's nest you have created for yourself now, Mr Austerley?"

"Where is she?" asked Kirkgordon.

"With Farthington, Mr Kirkgordon. She requires vengeance. And now he knows you're coming and he has his powerful ally back. Good work, Mr Austerley, you played the devil's hand." The priest turned away, head down.

"Great Austerley, just great. And no, don't say anything else. Just get ready. Havers needs us." Kirkgordon turned to Father Jonah.

"Father, I think you should stay and maintain the sanctuary you've set up. Just in case it all goes wrong."

"It's good of you to think of all those trapped people of Dillingham," answered the priest, "but if you fail, I'm not strong enough to deal with it all on my own. No, I shall go. Besides, this is Arthur we are talking about."

"Arthur? How well do you know him?"

"Too well. So many times we stood side by side. Those days may be gone and we may see things from very different angles these days but he was and still is my friend. I won't leave him to suffer."

Before Kirkgordon could ask anything further, Father Jonah hurried away, citing preparations to be made. Well, thought Kirkgordon, with Havers gone and Calandra elsewhere, Father Jonah's counsel may be just what's needed.

From his upstairs window, Mr Allison, erstwhile neighbour-hood watcher and general guardian of his street, looked down at the church car park. Over the last few days he had seen all sorts of strange goings on and numerous ghosts and creatures congregating around the grounds of the buildings. He had also been trapped within his own house, which was something, as soon as he was free, he would be taking up with the relevant authorities.

Now he was outraged at the complete disregard for driving safety that was occurring in the car park. First, a middle-aged man hobbled over to the electric car and got into the back seat. He was followed by that strange priest, whose smile Mr Allison had never trusted, holding a large staff, which clearly should have been stowed in the boot of the vehicle. Then some Robin Hood clown, complete with large bow and quiver, climbed into the passenger seat and failed to put on his seat belt. But what finally drove Mr Allison to reach for paper and pen was the priest's young daughter getting into the driver's seat and driving the car away.

The car glided without sound along the streets of Dillingham, which looked deserted. There were still people looking out of their windows, but no ghosts and no creatures could be seen.

"Did you destroy the creatures, Austerley, when you had your hands on Tania?" asked Kirkgordon.

"No. I couldn't. They are real creatures and although she has links to them they are not formed from her. They were real creatures to begin with. It's strange they aren't about."

Not good, Kirkgordon told himself. "Nefol, park up a good distance away. I have a nasty feeling we'll have some company before we reach Farthington."

Nefol nodded and was almost casual, looking out of the window at the fiery sky as she drove. Selecting a cul-de-sac off the main road to the care home, Nefol parked the car and jumped out. Kirkgordon stepped out and checked his quiver and bow, reciting some of the colours on the flashings and the arrows' uses. He watched Nefol grab the large staff and begin to twirl it. The ends turned white and all Kirkgordon could see was a blur.

"I've got a friend with a weapon just like that," said Kirkgordon to the priest. Father Jonah laughed and shook his head.

"Mr Kirkgordon, you are a simple one. You don't seriously believe that Havers gives Calandra two weeks off every month? It's been less than a month's total training time but Nefol's learnt so much from her. I should thank you. Havers said you gave Calandra back her self-worth. Most men would have stolen her beauty."

I must be the only one in the dark, Kirkgordon thought to himself. He told Austerley to stay with the priest while he scouted the territory ahead with Nefol. Jumping through the hedgerows and back gardens, Kirkgordon noticed how Nefol responded to his actions in a similar fashion to Calandra. He could see her influence. And he sorely wished she was here.

As they drew closer to the care home, Kirkgordon could see a variety of creatures patrolling the grounds. There was an elephant with the head of a crocodile and a viper for a tail. Hovering before the door was a giant wasp with a monkey's head. An enormous slug had a scorpion's tail and the legs of a cricket.

Beyond the animal freak show was a sight that chilled Kirkgordon's blood. Hanging by his hands, tied with a rope hooked around a weather vane on the roof, was Havers. His pain was obvious as he tried to lift himself up and not merely dangle. Underneath, taunting him, was Tania, now dressed in a black garment covered in symbols.

"He doesn't look in a good way," said Nefol.

"No," replied Kirkgordon. "Bring your father and Austerley up here. We move now!"

The Battle of Gibbet Point

Wilson exited the manhole of the sewer ahead of Jane Goodritch and scanned the street while lending a supporting arm. Jane breathed deeply, trying to expel the stench of the underground route from her too-sensitive nostrils.

"Did we really have to travel via the sewers?" asked Jane.

"Well, Miss Goodritch, many of the bizarre creatures we have seen recently have wings, as does Farthington himself. This was a way of keeping our intentions hidden. Hopefully the dragon doesn't know we're on to his shield device," explained Wilson.

"So it should be plain sailing."

"Never say that, Miss Goodritch."

"Why? And you can call me Jane, by the way."

"Well, Jane, Farthington will know that if we can disable his shield he's going to have a bucketful of SETAA agents on to him and possibly the boys from the military too. I don't see him risking that without having some sort of protective device around it."

"Good job we brought some extra weapons then." Jane held her machete pair aloft. Explorer blood was pumping in her veins and she was ready to take a stand for the good and the decent. In moments like this, on the move, Jane believed she could do this forever. But deep within she was haunted; there were moments when everything stopped and the true horror of it all sunk in.

Wilson was the picture of professionalism, pointing out the safe direction to Jane before breaking ahead to assess the next blind spot. From time to time he would glance up at the sky, but he couldn't see anything overhead. His ribs still hurt and he knew he wasn't at full fighting fitness, but he was upright, and at times like this that was the standard for duty.

"We're making good time, Jane," said Wilson as they reached the bottom of the climb to Gibbet Point. "We should take a break so that we're rested in case we have to fight."

Jane nodded and sat down. Wilson drew a bottle from his hip and offered her a drink. She gulped down the warm water eagerly and handed the bottle back. Sitting there, readying himself for duty, Wilson looked quite the hunk to her. He was obviously dedicated; she could see he had a care beyond himself. Her stomach felt light and she began to blush. Oh, what the hell, she thought.

"Wilson, see, when all this is over..." Jane took a deep breath. "Do you think you and me... that's us... could we get a drink together? Just a wee drink, nothing elaborate."

Wilson looked deep into her eyes and took her hands in his own. For a moment, he looked beyond Jane, towards the target they would soon reach. Then he looked back at her and nodded.

"Why not, Jane? Why not? You're a brave woman, very dedicated. It's quite intoxicating."

Jane grinned inanely at having bagged her saviour for a drink. She basked in Wilson's smile until he glanced again at the summit of the hill. His eyes narrowed and his smile faded. He scanned his target for a full minute before returning his gaze to her face.

"Stay safe, Jane Goodritch, stay safe. Whatever happens up there, stay safe behind me." Jane nodded and dropped her head. He caught it with his hand, tilted her head back and delivered a passionate kiss. She tingled inside. It had been so long, and her body was not the shape it had once been. This moment needed to last.

But then her saviour announced it was time for the attack on the shield generator at the summit. Reluctantly Jane stood, machetes in hand, half a step back from Wilson. At least she could be on his shoulder.

The climb was steep and difficult, especially as they were avoiding the path, but Jane was determined not to be left behind. Wilson barely turned around, his eyes constantly scanning the terrain ahead. Without warning he dropped down, grabbing her shirt, forcing her to the ground with him.

The tiger's body stood out against the greenery but the toad's head did not. The snake heads waving at the rear hissed unkindly. Wilson drew his wooden clubs. Jane had seen Havers use these and she was surprised to see them again.

"Arthur had those, too. Are they standard issue?"

"No, but he did teach me how to fight, and what to fight with," said Wilson, grinning. "I hope there's just one of those," he added, nodding towards the tiger-toad.

Wilson waited for the creature to stalk away from him and then clambered further up the hill. Jane tailed him as closely as she could until he sent her off in a different direction. She lay flat on the grass and waited for his signal. She had seen such weird creatures recently that this hybrid didn't shock her as much as the previous ones had. The toad-headed creature came past Wilson again and he chose this time to attack. The snakes hissed a warning but he slammed his arm down on the tail and bludgeoned it off with two blows. The creature turned; Wilson leapt onto its back and began to beat it severely. Within five seconds, Wilson had broken its back and the creature was subdued.

Jane ran up the hill towards the swinging cage, the source of the shield, and reached out with her machetes, ready to cut it down. As she approached she felt an almighty force erupt against her midriff as if she had been kicked. Falling backwards, she broke her fall with her hands but let her machetes drop in the process. Wilson, running her way, was caught by an invisible arm, clothes-lining and dropping him to the grass beneath. Jane couldn't understand what had happened. Something rolled Wilson onto his front and drove into his back, causing him to cry out in pain. Jane watched in frustrated horror, seeing her new love being pummelled by something that wasn't even there.

There was a brief moment of panic before Jane's reflexes kicked in. She picked herself up and ran towards Wilson. Her brain said that whatever was pounding his back must be stood directly over him. Arms outstretched and ready to shove, Jane attacked, but before she felt any contact, a hand grabbed her throat and lifted her into the air. Feet dangling, she grabbed at the invisible hands that held her, desperately trying to prise them open but to no avail.

Wilson was groggy but still conscious. He saw Jane suspended in the air and fought the reaction to merely lash out at her attacker, whatever and wherever it was. He would need a smarter plan than that. Rolling quickly to one side, Wilson made for a rock he had seen in the grass. It looked just over the size of his fist and was the only weapon he could see. His sticks were on the far side of the invisible creature and he wanted to keep the being's focus on Jane. His sides screamed out with every roll but he forced himself to keep going.

Gripping the rock with his strong arm, Wilson looked at Jane, her face trying to scream out but lacking the air to do it. There were indentations on her throat made by fingers unseen, and the colour in her face was draining. Her air supply had been cut off and she was looking straight through her attacker, her eyes begging Wilson for help.

It should be right there. If I was holding someone in a choke, then surely I would be right there, thought Wilson. He desperately looked for some sort of confirmation, knowing time was against him. If the creature stopped focusing on Jane then all was lost. And then he found what he was looking for. Yes! The indentations on the grass. There were three distinct impressions. Not long and foot-like, more like a very thick pole sitting on the ground. A tri-ped? Wilson didn't know anything about those. Oh hell, he cried to himself. And then he threw the rock right at Jane's face.

She couldn't move to avoid it. Hurtling towards her was a large stone and part of Jane thought it might just end the pain quicker when it hit. Instinctively her eyes closed but her ears heard the thud ahead of her. Wilson saw a wild splodge of green liquid jettisoned from empty air, a spontaneous fountain that began to cover Jane. The grip on Jane's throat was released and she stumbled backwards, her eyes closed as the green fluid continued to spray.

Wilson watched the spraying liquid and saw the impressions on the ground begin to move. He realized the creature was coming for him. The impressions on the ground moved closer and Wilson looked around for another weapon.

"Jane, get the sticks! Get me my sticks!"

Jane was wiping the putrid green fluid from her eyes. She looked around for the sticks; the nearest one was only a few feet away. She grabbed it and stumbled towards Wilson. He was screaming. Jane could see that both of his shoulders were pinned to the ground with his eyes fixated on the space above him. Six feet up, the green fluid continued to spray.

Wilson knew there was a third appendage and guessed it was hovering above his head, about to smack down on his forehead, sending him to oblivion. All the time he was carefully watching the position of the fluid, waiting for it to dip as the appendage struck. It dipped. Wilson threw his head and neck as far to one side as he could. Something caught the corner of his neck and pinned it to the floor. He was still alive, barely.

Jane came barrelling into the figure over Wilson. She couldn't see it but it was obvious it was standing over him. Hitting one of its legs, Jane felt it give but she bounced off to one side, dropping the stick beside Wilson. A large indentation appeared on the ground; the creature must have fallen over. With no hesitation, Wilson grabbed the stick, summoned all his remaining reserves and leapt on top of the creature. The creature's skin was coarse and Wilson could feel little abrasions forming all over his body. Ignoring this, Wilson repeated the same action over and over again, taking his stick and pounding the area that the green fluid was coming from.

Jane was willing him on to eliminate the creature, but she felt revulsion as Wilson's face contorted with rage and vengeance. He battered away at the creature until his strength gave in and he collapsed back, rolling off the green mess that was left. She had known he could be destructive but it had always been controlled: smooth and effective, brave and defensive.

She understood the rage, having herself been throttled by the creature, but she was still shocked at the ferocity of Wilson's outpouring of hate. Picking herself up and going over to him, she caught his eye, but he dropped his gaze and looked away from her, as if he knew she had seen his darkest of sides. And then his eyes closed. His chest still moved with his breathing, but it was slowing.

No, she thought, I can't lose you, not now, not when we've just survived. No. I won't let it. Jane embraced Wilson and cried over him.

"What to do, what do I do?" she said out loud, composing herself. "Airways, breathing, circulation. Need to check his airway." Jane pulled Wilson's mouth apart and pushed two fingers down. Wilson coughed violently before telling her, through the choking, to leave him alone.

"I'm good. Jane... I'm good. Cage... the cage."

"Don't worry about that. I'll take care of you, I'll sort you out, you're going nowhere." Jane held him close, arms wrapped around him. "Don't talk. Just relax."

"Jane," said Wilson in a harsh croak. "Destroy... the cage... or the... others... will be dead."

Care Home Chaos

The elephant-crocodile looks the most dangerous," Kirkgordon told Nefol. The girl nodded, placed a hand into his quiver and removed an arrow.

"That's the one for the little guys with the hammers, yes?" Nefol nodded. "Good, positions then."

It had not been an easy decision to disperse his group but Kirkgordon was worried that Farthington and Tania were nowhere to be seen. Nefol was to attack from his far right, with Austerley beside Kirkgordon and the priest on the far left. Kirkgordon wasn't sure what help Father Jonah would be but he had taken a large mace with him which wouldn't be of use to someone without training, so Kirkgordon guessed he was probably pretty handy.

Kirkgordon drew back his bow and let loose an arrow at the elephant part. The arrow speared the flank of the creature. Immediately, tiny men with miniature hammers appeared from it, working with frenzy and driving the beast to its knees. Father Jonah emerged from his cover and cried aloud at the wasp-monkey, which turned from its lazy path to fly directly towards the priest. Nefol ran at the slug-scorpion, which sprang into the air, landing behind her. And Austerley... where the hell is the idiot, wondered Kirkgordon.

A knife appeared at his throat from nowhere. He had been compromised. What was happening? Then he felt the evil sweet breath on his neck.

"I like a man who knows how to fire an arrow." Tania was behind him. He felt her lean into him, her chest pressing against his back and a leg snaking around his own. Glancing down, he saw only a stump where the foot should have been but was distracted by a hand reaching between his legs and stroking his thigh.

"You can still be mine. I can sense you still want me, still want to take me as your own." The hand moved higher up his thigh. The arms had sleeves on them, black and shiny with ornate symbols that were totally lost on Kirkgordon. Well at least she's not naked again, reasoned Kirkgordon. He could feel himself stirring below even though he was fighting not to become aroused. Her hand moved even higher. Now that's just not fair, he thought.

"Then take the knife away," he said. "Or don't you have enough trust in your womanly charms? Afraid I won't respond? Afraid you don't have enough to convince me?" Kirkgordon was beginning to sweat as the knife pressed harder into his throat.

"I know you're responding, I can feel it," laughed Tania in his ear. Damn, thought Kirkgordon, that feels too good.

"Why are you working with Farthington? Why not come with me and we'll get away from here? A fresh start, Tania. Just you and me."

"I don't think you mean that. I think you're just playing me. You'll never leave your other woman."

"Why? You think I won't. I've got all I want in you. And I want all of it. You can feel that, can't you? Feel my hunger."

"I want to taste your hunger." Tania pressed the knife harder, forcing Kirkgordon's head to turn, and bit his lips in a playful fashion. He responded by engulfing her mouth, deeply tasting her. Oblivious to everything else, the couple tasted each other. Tania dropped the knife, allowing Kirkgordon to turn around and take hold of her hips. Stepping back, he looked at her in her skin-tight black dress; she was revealing an obscene amount of cleavage. He drew a sharp breath. Playing this close to the edge was difficult but Tania was starting to succumb.

"Come with me, let me take you back to the church, and we'll plan what we'll do." Her eyes were full of passion but the witchy wildness that had been so dominant before had died. There was a new calm about her. Tania started to apologize, saying that she had done it all for him. She had looked into her future and she had seen Kirkgordon in the water and she had wanted him. And the old practices had taught her how to do it. But now she would win him on her own, without compulsion.

Kirkgordon smiled to reassure her and, for the first time, noticed she was hovering just above the ground. Now that's a trick that Austerley could have done with, he thought. Then he saw the lumbering figure appear behind Tania. Before he could shout a warning, Austerley swung a small sword at Tania's neck.

Austerley had never been a man of weapons and his mastery of them failed to improve with this strike. The blade was swung so inexpertly that he struck Tania's neck with the flat side, merely bruising her. Watching Tania's face, Kirkgordon saw the rage develop and the wildness return to her eyes.

"Liar! Betrayer!" she screamed at Kirkgordon. She twisted her hands into a convoluted form and reached towards Auster- ley. His smaller foot flew into the air and his body seemed to hang from it. Tania spun the university professor round and round until he became a blur. When she finally let him go, Austerley sailed through the air and crashed into a set of trees. She turned to confront Kirkgordon but he was gone.

Racing through some undergrowth, all Kirkgordon could think was how that stupid arse had screwed it all up again. And she'll be wild now, wild. Judging by what she's just done to Indy, she's going to be quite a handful. Glancing over at his other compatriots, he saw that Nefol had engaged the slug creature and the priest was striking the wasp concoction with a hefty blow from his mace. But something beyond that caught his eye. Many would have thought it to be another piecemeal creature, but Kirkgordon had seen those three heads before. Each head had one eye closed, damaged beyond repair by an arrow from Kirkgordon's bow back on that dreadful island. He's going to be pissed about that, thought Kirkgordon.

"Time to bring out the side shows," Kirkgordon called to Father Jonah, before drawing his bow and firing an arrow into the wasp. A one-eyed giant appeared and began swatting at the wasp with his club. The wasp flew off, high into the air, and then dived at great speed and stung the giant on its head. A howl split the air that would have drowned out a football crowd, and the giant went into a berserker rage. The wasp was swiped aside with one blow. The next blow hit the slug and sent wet slime in all directions. It jumped some thirty feet on its cricket legs but the giant chased it down and pounded its wounded body. The slug lashed out with its scorpion tail but it missed the giant, who continued to batter the slimy creature until it no longer moved.

The giant at the care home had looked for direction from Kirkgordon but this time the magical beast ran straight for

Farthington. The giant was nearly as tall as the dragon but Farthington was three times as wide. As the giant attacked Farthington with his club raised, the dragon caught him in the stomach with a solid foot. It was less like a kick and more like a brick wall being erected. The giant collided with the foot and dropped down to the ground.

Kirkgordon saw Farthington take to the air and he knew what was coming next. He drew a vortex arrow and fired it off as one of the dragon's heads blew fire over the giant. Another head sent a fireball onto the arrow and it burned to a black crisp. The fire from the first head subsided and Kirkgordon saw his giant's burnt husk lying on the ground. It was a strange feeling, a loss of what was effectively only a weapon, but Kirkgordon felt as though something of his had died. His professional core fought the rage seeping in.

"Enough of this... how do you say in this country... dross!" roared Farthington, his other heads adding to the mocking laughter. Kirkgordon drew another arrow but the air in front of him turned black. It was like a power cut at midnight with the moon turning its back out of spite. The blackness was thick. Kirkgordon heard a voice in his ear.

"Toy with me, would you? Play me for a fool? When I have offered everything, you mock me, tease me with your longing for me. I will make you suffer, I will make you curse the day you were born a man." It was Tania's voice but there was a hollowness to it, as if her soul had gone, leaving the merest essence of the girl she had been.

Something hit Kirkgordon right between his legs, knocking him off his feet and making his eyes water. His genitalia screamed in pain and he had to force himself to roll away. The next blow caught him on his backside while he was face down in his roll: a fortunate result, for his genitals had once again been the target.

Light exploded into the darkness and created an illuminated shell within which all could be seen. Outside of this area, the shroud persisted; nothing could be seen, not even shadow. The priest was standing over Kirkgordon, toe to floating toe with Tania. Kirkgordon watched in horror as small insects, all jet black but with little pincers at their front, began to pour out of Tania's ears, eyes and mouth. They jumped from Tania onto Father Jonah and within a few seconds they had covered the priest. Nearly vomiting, Kirkgordon reached for an arrow but the priest, still covered in insects, reached out with his hand held aloft.

Watching in disbelief, Kirkgordon saw the insects begin to change colour from black to grey before turning completely white. Without warning, every single insect leapt from the priest onto Tania, covering her completely, and she toppled to the ground.

"Do you have any vortex arrows left, Mr Kirkgordon?" asked the priest. Kirkgordon indicated an affirmative. "Then over there, ten feet beside the witch. Fire one now!"

Kirkgordon drew his bow and fired the arrow into the ground ten feet from Tania. The vortex started to build and the priest bowed his head. Kirkgordon saw others being drawn towards the rupture in space, but as the priest started to move it was like a wall had been placed in front of him. Tania and Nefol were not moving either. But Farthington was. The dragon roared and turned his back to the phenomenon then pushed hard with his legs and flapped his mighty wings to try and escape its pull. Despite these efforts, he was gradually being drawn towards it.

The insects covering Tania turned black again, crawling like a mass of ants all over her body. Not a part of her skin could be seen. And then, almost as one, they were whipped off her body and disappeared into the vortex, vanishing before Kirkgordon's eyes. The priest remained motionless, his hair and gown blowing towards the vanishing point. Farthington was still slipping backwards but was gaining more purchase as the vortex began to die.

As the winds faded, Kirkgordon saw that the priest's face looked weary and drained. Father Jonah turned his eyes towards Tania and a smile spread across his face. Tania looked almost peaceful, lying in her black outfit but with renewed radiance in her face. This development exhilarated Kirkgordon, but he had to temper his joy and survey the scene to see what Farthington was about to do next.

"Take Tania and get her out of here," Father Jonah ordered Kirkgordon. Without hesitation, Kirkgordon swept Tania up in his arms and began to run for cover.

"No you don't!" The voice was incredibly loud and full of rage. Kirkgordon turned his head to see one of Farthington's mouths swinging towards him. Fire raged from the orifice before Kirkgordon could react, and the heat reached him in an instant. So sure was he that the flames would overwhelm him, just as they had overwhelmed his giant, that Kirkgordon didn't even turn away. But, to his amazement, while the oppressive heat of the flames reached him, the actual flames broke around him as if he were in a protective shell.

It took a moment for Kirkgordon to comprehend his situation. Through the flames he saw the priest, arms raised out towards Kirkgordon, somehow repelling the flames. But Farthington wasn't to be beaten and the second head sent out flames, this time aimed towards Nefol. Again, Father Jonah reached out a hand, and the flames split around her. By now the priest was buckling and he dropped to his knees. Farthington, sensing weakness, turned his third head and poured flames onto the priest. The flames broke just before the priest, and the fire started to close in on Kirkgordon and Nefol, the heat beginning to singe their clothes.

The priest looked towards Nefol and said something. Kirkgordon didn't hear but he saw Nefol's face fall. Father Jonah turned to him.

"Kirkgordon, Nefol was my daughter. She is now yours. Look after my child."

Kirkgordon's heart sank and his face became pained. The priest called out at the top of his voice and pushed his arms out sideways, one towards Kirkgordon and one towards Nefol. The girl screamed and Kirkgordon felt the heat around him begin to fade. He saw the fire being driven away from himself and Nefol, but the flames were encroaching on the priest and he began to burn. With one last surge he drove his arms outwards again. The fire from the two heads attacking Kirkgordon and Nefol turned back towards the heads, setting the heads themselves on fire. Farthington started to fall from the sky. But the remaining flames had engulfed Father Jonah, and when the flames eventually ceased, there was nothing left of the priest.

Nefol dropped to her knees, tears streaming from her face. The shock of the priest's death froze Kirkgordon to the spot. Only the sight of Farthington rolling on the ground brought Kirkgordon back to his senses. Tania was out cold. He ran to the foliage and set her down in the bushes. On his left, Kirkgordon saw Austerley stumbling along, dazed, and a little confused. Then all light disappeared. Out of the darkness, a voice spoke.

"Who's going to save you now, Austerley? I can see in the

dark, without any help from your charcoaled priest. Can you?"

In The Dark

Jane Goodritch moved to destroy the cage but was suddenly plunged into complete darkness. She fell and landed with a thud on the ground, hurting her shoulder. A feeling of utter disorientation set in. Jane tried to think where she was on the hill top, aware that there was a cliff edge close at hand.

"Wilson, I can't see. I can't blinking well see. I don't know where the cage is," she yelled at the top of her lungs.

In a soft throaty whisper, Wilson replied, "Jane, calm down, just calm down. I know where I am. I'll guide you but you need to listen. Be calm love, just be calm."

Jane nodded and then realized nobody could see anything. "Of course," she answered.

"Good. Now, I want you to count slowly and with an even volume. First I will bring you to me. Slowly and evenly, okay?" Jane didn't acknowledge but instead began her count.

"One. Two. Three. Four. One. Two ..."

"Good, but more even with your volume, it's very important." The count continued but with less variation in volume. "Better. Now we're going to move. Take two steps in your current direction." Jane moved and kept counting. "About turn and then four steps." The process continued until Jane tripped over Wilson.

"Good, good, you're here. Now stand and let me feel your feet. Good. Turn this way a bit. Okay, that's a direct line, but you still need to count. I'll tell you if you go off line."

Jane stepped forward slowly. Twice, Wilson corrected her movement, but after a short while she knew she was close to the edge of the cliff as the wind rose slightly into her face. Any movement now could take her off the cliff.

"Wilson, I'm close, very close. I'm nearly over the edge," she shrieked.

"Calm. Stay calm and count. Trust me, Jane. Trust me."

She continued with Wilson's instructions until she felt her foot slip. She fell forward and panicked, believing that her descent was unstoppable. Just as she reached out, her fingers clutched something made of metal. Her hands gripped the cage and she swung out. A gust of wind from below told her she was over the cliff and she clung on desperately.

"I've got it," gasped Jane, "Wilson, I've got it!"

"Then pull down. Pull down with everything."

"But I'll be off the cliff! I'm swinging over the edge."

"Let your feet down, Jane. Just slowly let your feet down."

Swinging back and forth, Jane started to let her feet down and her ankles cracked off the edge of the cliff. Jane winced but at least she now knew where the cliff edge was. After the next swing she planted two feet on the ground and pulled hard. The cage was heavy and it was dragging her towards the edge of the cliff in the darkness. The momentum was building. If it didn't come free soon, it would drag her over the edge. Just as she was deciding whether she needed to remount the cage or let go and prepare for its brutal return swing, the metal device broke loose of its chain.

Jane dropped off the cage and threw herself backwards to

try to avoid toppling over the cliff. Her toes felt the edge and her feet slid off into nothingness. Using all her will and sense of self-preservation, she managed to turn as she fell. She scraped at the ground with her hands. In the dark she fought for purchase as several nails broke from her efforts. As her body followed her feet over the edge, her left hand grabbed on to a rock and her right hand snatched at a piece of gorse. With the spikes biting into her hand, Jane held on, clinging to the meagre supports.

"Wilson," she screamed, "I'm slipping. Wilson, help me!"

Jane heard the cage falling down the cliff. One thud, then another, followed by an almighty clatter. Her eyes were suddenly blinded by pure, natural light. As her sight returned, she saw a hand reaching towards her. Her own hand on the rock was slipping. Wilson grabbed hold of her arm. Jane gripped tighter on to the gorse, ignored the pain and pulled hard with both arms.

The gorse slipped loose and tumbled down her left side. Jane was dangling over the cliff by one hand. Desperately she tried to swing her free hand up towards the cliff edge, but she was losing her grip and began to slip. The hand holding her gripped tighter, stopping her slide. Looking below, Jane saw the drop and the waves crashing against the rocks. Her hand slipped further. So this was it. Time to check out. And she blacked out.

Wilson held on in agony. His arm was screaming at him and the feeling in his hands was beyond pain, but he kept gripping. She was going to go, about to tumble to her doom. This was it. All or nothing. He steeled himself for the white hot complaints his body would register and he rolled away from the edge, pulling Jane's arm with all his might, desperately trying to drag her over the cliff top. A weight landed on his upturned body, bringing more pain. But this time he welcomed it. And he lay there, forcing a smile through the agony that was caused by Jane Goodritch lying on top of him.

Austerley spun round in the dark, searching for the source of the sound. Now that he had a smaller foot, he was unsteady and hesitant with his steps. The last time Farthington and Austerley had come face to face, the dragon had ripped his foot off; now that he was a biped again, Austerley was keen to remain that way. Kneeling down, he touched the tarmac with his hands and chanted a series of low droning noises.

"There you are, Austerley. Crouching down. Are you begging for mercy? You'll find none. I would have had all the money in the world, Austerley. Dagon's right-hand dragon. But no, you couldn't do the one thing I required of you. So now you'll suffer. I'll pin you down and rip off your other foot. Then your fingers, then your arms. And when there are no limbs left I'll snap your neck and toss your worthless torso to the crows. I see you shaking, Austerley. I smell your fear."

Austerley's body was trembling but he kept his focus on the tarmac. The language he uttered was old, from a village deep in a rainforest. He had seen their practices and he knew their ways could shock even those who had dealt with the bloody horror of a night in the wildest of cities. This was power and he was its master. The tarmac cracked.

Kirkgordon felt the ground move. The surface of the care home's car park pulled out from under him like a rug. Kirkgordon lost his footing and tumbled in the dark. He heard Nefol yelp. He rolled until he hit something hard. Reaching out with his hand, he felt the bark of a tree. Disorientated, he listened to try to figure out what was happening.

A roar reverberated, a cry of frustration. Farthington's

large feet were thumping on the ground and possibly kicking at something. Kirkgordon heard a crack and something hit the tree just above his head. Reaching up, he felt a piece of tarmac. Bemused, he rolled to one side, thinking he may have inadvertently ended up in a line of attack.

Kirkgordon's eyes blinked shut as natural daylight flooded the scene. Jane and Wilson had succeeded! Straining to take in the scene before him, he saw only a huge black blob. As his eyes adjusted, he saw a giant man-shaped piece of tarmac throwing a right hook at Farthington. Behind the tarmac man was Austerley, kneeling on the ground, deep in concentration. Seeing that Farthington was completely occupied with the tarmac man, Kirkgordon took the chance to look for his goal, Havers. The government agent was still swinging on the end of a rope and Kirkgordon took an ordinary arrow from his quiver.

For a moment, as he looked along the arrow, everything drifted away. Kirkgordon let his breathing slow down. He relaxed and let the fingers of the hand gripping his bow ease off. His eye saw the target perfectly; he simply released the drawstring and watched his arrow fly. With years of practice behind him, he turned away, knowing it would hit his target. A smug smile came across his face as he heard Havers thump to the ground.

"Nefol," Kirkgordon said to the girl, "get over to Havers and protect him." The girl raced off but to Kirkgordon's horror she ran directly at Farthington. "No, don't engage him. Nefol, no!"

Kirkgordon immediately saw the change in Nefol, who was normally so cool and calm. She fought with rage, and her normal technique of avoiding contact, stepping past her enemy's blows and counter-attacking was lost in her fury. She approached the dragon head-on like an irate wrestler. Farthington had spotted her coming. She piled straight into his upturned foot and collapsed to the ground. The dragon lifted his foot to crush her but was jumped on by the tarmac man, who began to pummel him.

"Crush him, Mr Austerley! Eliminate the filth!" Kirkgordon knew the voice but the wrath contained within it was unusual for the normally cool Havers. Racing over to Nefol, Kirkgordon could see she was breathing but badly hurt.

The dragon cried out as the tarmac man beat it to a pulp. "I have Alana!" The name froze Kirkgordon's heart.

"Austerley, stop!" ordered Kirkgordon.

"He took my foot. He took my bloody foot, the bastard, I'll kill him!" yelled Austerley. His arms were making the same pounding motion as the tarmac man.

"I have your Alana. She's dead if I don't return!" roared Farthington.

"Dispatch him, Austerley," encouraged Havers. "End your pain."

He could be bluffing, thought Kirkgordon, but if not, dear God... I can't lose her. The kids need her. They can't lose her. Alana, no!

Austerley felt the tip of the arrow on his head and heard the voice saying, "Stop it now. Stop that creature of yours, now!" Kirkgordon's voice was calm but urgent.

"That bastard dragon's gonna pay, Churchy!"

A trickle of blood ran down the side of Austerley's head as the arrow tip was forced slightly deeper. "Now, or I will kill you."

Looking deep into Kirkgordon's eyes, Austerley saw a man of sheer intent. His rage died in the face of self-preservation.

"Mr Kirkgordon, I order you to stop this and let Mr Austerley do his work to eliminate our threat. Step aside, Mr Kirkgordon."

"That's my family! Havers, interfere now and I will hunt you down. Let the dragon speak!" raged Kirkgordon.

"I will not. You cannot trust this beast. It's a trick and I will finish him now." Havers, walking slowly after his torture, limped towards Farthington. Caught between holding Austerley at bay and stopping Havers, Kirkgordon was outnumbered and at a loss. A smile broke across Havers' lips and he prepared to dispatch the dragon. A whirring sound went unnoticed by all those on the ground except for Nefol.

"If I die, she dies. Kirkgordon, they need to hear from me." Farthington's voice was becoming agitated and the dragon's face showed panic at Havers' approach.

Kirkgordon bowed his head, feeling at a loss. Any arrow would be pointless. He'd have to hit Havers, which, given the distance and the target, was unlikely to succeed. It would also free up Austerley to reinitiate the fight. Hollowness and shame at his weakness filled him. Alana's face filled his mind and he began to break down inside.

Kirkgordon's breakdown was interrupted by the whoosh of large black wings and then a cry of "This is all a bit serious, boys!"

Calandra, her skin cold and white, dressed in black boots, jeans and leather jacket, dropped down beside Farthington. Kirkgordon gawped at her.

"Glad you could join us, my dear," said Havers. "We have been busy and now it's time to settle our scores. This is for Ohlos!" said Havers as he advanced once again towards the dragon.

"Farthington's got Alana, Cally! Stop Havers!" shouted Kirkgordon.

Calandra's staff upended Havers and pinned him to the ground.

"I think you forget, my dear, you are on my payroll," Havers pointed out.

"Time to speak, Farthington," ordered Kirkgordon, "or I'll let Havers back up."

The dragon let go a sigh of relief, expelling air, and began to shake. Having seen Farthington change from human to dragon, Kirkgordon always thought he wouldn't be surprised if he saw the opposite change. He was wrong. It was like watching a bizarre nature film in reverse as the beast was packed into a shell too small to contain it.

Lying beneath Austerley's tarmac creature, Farthington's human form produced a mobile phone from his garments, which had appeared on him out of nowhere as he shrunk. With the words "Put her on", Farthington switched on loudspeaker mode and held the phone up.

For Kirkgordon, at this distance, the voice was faint but unmistakeable. It was Alana.

"C, do what they say. They have me. I don't know where I am but it's weird. Things I have never seen before. Help me, help me!"

Farthington switched off the mobile. "Time I was going," he said.

"Austerley, let him go."

There was a moment's hesitation then Austerley felt the arrow point press in on his head. Releasing his hands from the ground, he muttered a few words and the tarmac creature broke apart over Farthington, who stood up and shook himself down. Taking a piece of chalk from his pocket, he drew a complex symbol on the ground and stood on it.

"So nice to see you all again. Don't follow me!" And he vanished into the ground. Havers, lying on his back, knocked Calandra's staff aside and made as quick a pace as he could to the symbol.

"Follow him! We need to follow him."

Just as he reached the spot on the ground, a nightgaunt, a jet black creature with wings, legs, torso and head but no eyes or mouth, sprang out of the hole. It rubbed the symbol away before flying off into the sky.

"You," said Havers, pointing at Kirkgordon. "You let him go. You'll accompany me back to HQ and we'll sort out how you follow orders."

Kirkgordon completely ignored Havers and called Calandra to him.

"Did you hear me, Kirkgordon?" asked Havers.

"Excuse me, but there is a fatherless child that needs us. As for you and your games, don't even speak to me. Just don't speak."

Back in the USSR

"Do you remember the last time? We damn well near got roasted." Calandra had her hand on Kirkgordon's shoulder and could feel the tension. Gently she rubbed the muscles that ran to the base of his neck. To many others this would have seemed like the touch of a would-be lover but she tried to see the relationship more like sister and brother. Calandra saw how he looked at her at times, with a hunger that she felt too, but his choice of partner was always Alana. And now Alana was a hostage and Calandra would help him win her back.

"Too well, Cally, too well. Always hauling Austerley's fat arse around." Kirkgordon spat on the ground and surveyed the Russian countryside. He remembered the place far too well. It was here that Farthington had first revealed himself as Zmey Gorynych, the dragon. Here, where a car door had been the only thing between Austerley and himself and a rapid cremation. And here where Calandra, after fighting off many nightgaunts, had provided an exit by drawing that peculiar symbol on the ground.

"How did you know the exit was still open?" Calandra continued to rub his shoulders, the knots evident.

Thinking back, Kirkgordon could still visualize the nightgaunts emerging from the portal and racing to attack Calandra and himself. "Havers. He spoke to the FSB, who had kept an eye on it. Many things have come out of it since and they reckon it's an active doorway. Well, we'll find out." Kirkgordon stared at the exit. He had seen his children only briefly before leaving them in the care of Alana's mother. Someone has Mum. That was all he had told them. How could you explain all this nonsense anyway? Some things should be kept quiet, under the cover of government.

Havers had been awkward. The callous swine would have let Alana die to keep the whole thing quiet. But Kirkgordon had called "Ma'am", SETAA's real head. Her Majesty had understood that it may have been possible to silence Kirkgordon, but not before he could deliver enough evidence to the press to blow SETAA wide open. Kirkgordon was sure he detected some strain in her voice as "Ma'am" explained to Havers that Kirkgordon would be the operational head of a rescue mission. But her backing was important. Havers, although a ruthless bastard, was better as a colleague than as an enemy.

"How's Nefol?" asked Kirkgordon.

"She's good to go," replied Calandra. "Poor girl took it hard, really hard. But she's focused, not vengeful. I'll keep her close to me, Churchy. She won't let you down." Calandra smiled at him. Her cold white flesh was hidden by her black jeans and leather jacket. He's so distant, she thought. Alana has seeped into his skin.

"Keep her close. Father Jonah saved my life. I owe it to him." Kirkgordon turned his eyes to the last member of his rescue squad. This one had taken a hell of a lot of persuading. "And how's my partner? Still a stupid arse?" Austerley swore at him.

Calandra gently kissed the back of Kirkgordon's neck. "Take

it easy, you know you need him." She heard him let out a breath, trying to release his anger at the man before him. "Austerley's been suffering too. The foot he stole from Tania has gone completely black. Plus it's smaller and unbalances him when he walks. I think, from what I know about the process he undertook, that some of Tania's darkness transferred across in the foot. Austerley took her foot before Father Jonah had a chance to cleanse her."

"So he's now not only a nut job but also possessed in some way?"

"That's a fair assumption."

"Are you sure I need him?"

"Yes!" Calandra turned Kirkgordon to face her and looked deep into his eyes. "Churchy, we'll get Alana back. If I have to rip hell apart, we'll get her back. But Austerley knows these places. I have spent time in the other worlds but he is a map, an encyclopaedia of the bad lands. With his contacts, we have a chance to find her."

Kirkgordon turned away but Calandra pulled him back. "Listen, Havers scoured the globe. I've seen him find anyone. He's the best, and he found nothing. Farthington must have her in the other places. So now we go to them and find her. But you need Austerley. He is our compass. But you're our captain. As for the rest of us, we're just firepower."

"I know," he said, looking straight at her, "and thank you. I know you would like me to think of you the same way I think of her. And if I wasn't with her I would be with you. So thank you."

A tear slipped out from Calandra's eye. It turned into a solid elongated piece of ice on her cheek.

"Black suits you, Cally. For someone so cold you look damn

hot!" He kissed her forehead before turning to the small fleet of cars behind him.

"Mr Kirkgordon, are you ready?" Just for a moment, Kirkgordon thought that it was Havers. Instead, Wilson stood dressed in an impeccable suit, complete with open overcoat and bowler hat. "It does get damn chilly here in the Russian motherland."

"Wilson! How's the body? You took some pasting back on the English coast."

There was just a momentary wince from the corner of his mouth before Wilson replied. "Tip top, sir, just tip top. Job to do, Queen and country, you know how it is. Besides, now that you are taking Major Havers with you, someone's got to run the department while he's gone. And do try not to piss him off in there. He's been like the proverbial bear with a sore head back at HQ."

"Well, I get that. He was very close to Father Jonah. I'd like nothing better than to take this dragon apart as well. Look, Wilson, thanks for organizing everything. I appreciate it. Havers has been a little cold since I spoke with your boss. Not used to little upstarts like myself."

"I am sure I don't need to remind you," said Wilson, reminding Kirkgordon, "that she's your boss too. All in the service of, my dear fellow, all in the service of."

"Speaking of which, how is Miss Goodritch?"

There was not a flicker, not one hint of emotion. "I believe Miss Goodritch is recovering well after her exertions. Got a lot to thank her for, both of us. I believe she's going to see Ma'am as well. Bit of the old keeping-it-under-the-nose conversation. I do believe Jane is quite excited." And there it was. Just the merest curling up of the corners of the lips, a momentary demonstration of warmth.

"How did you sort out Dillingham? I take it 'Ma'am' didn't pay everyone a visit," asked Kirkgordon.

"We have our ways, Mr Kirkgordon. Very convincing. You'd be surprised what you can achieve when everyone attends a town hall meeting."

"What, do you just like mind zap them all?"

"Really, Mr Kirkgordon, how very Hollywood. You sound like a regular film buff. No, we do not 'zap' them, but we have some very talented personnel who can reach out to the masses. A way with words, shall we say?"

Kirkgordon saw a number of black-suited men beyond Wilson's shoulder. From his years of protection work, Kirkgordon recognized the hardware beneath the jackets. "I take it they are not your people."

"Oh, no. Common park thugs, by the look of it. Our dear friends in the FSB, while being most helpful of course, do like to show a little muscle on home turf. I suppose it's their way of letting us know who is running the show. Well, as long as they think that, I guess it is all fine and dandy."

Kirkgordon stepped away to check over his equipment one more time. Father Jonah's cellar had been a mine of weaponry, and Kirkgordon now had a small backpack of items which he believed would prove extremely useful. Havers had tried to confiscate all the items but Kirkgordon had gone over his head to "Ma'am" again, building the icy wall between the two men even higher.

Satisfied that his pack was prepared, Kirkgordon slung it onto his back and approached Havers, who was talking to a bald man in military uniform with an array of medals hanging from his chest. Rather than engage whatever general Havers was talking to, Kirkgordon gave a small flick of his head indicating it was time to go.

The snow compacted beneath his boots. Kirkgordon relished the crunching sound, wondering if there would be any snow in the days ahead. He would be stepping into the dragon's den, so to speak, and he was uneasy at leaving this world, where he felt he had a slight advantage. Who was to know what was lurking through the portal?

Austerley! Austerley would know. Through all the troubles of his recent past there had been one constant: Austerley. He needed the oaf to find Alana, needed to forge a working relationship again. For the sake of his wife and his children's mother, he would once again have to partner and protect this madman. Walking over to Austerley, who sat on the snow looking at his new foot, Kirkgordon decided to reach out.

"Austerley, get off your fat arse and let's get going. I don't want you slowing us down." Oh well, thought Kirkgordon, looks like I'll need to work on my bonding techniques.

"It's black, like bloody ebony. Who knows what that damn witch gave me?" moaned Austerley to the world in general.

It really is black, mused Kirkgordon. Not like the skin of someone on the equator. No, this was black, like evil. Undiluted evil, screaming its filth at you.

"Get your sock on and your backside into gear. It's time to go."

Austerley swore but began to haul himself to his feet. Kirkgordon called his team around him and they dropped into a loose formation. Calandra and Nefol went ahead at point, then Kirkgordon and Austerley side by side, leaving Havers to watch their rear. There was a sense of pride in his team, Kirkgordon realized, for they were survivors. But now was the time to let their pride go. They were about to see entirely new vistas and they needed to be quick learners if they wanted to return home.

Getting close to the portal, he saw a swirling mass of what could be stars. Calandra turned her head, waiting for the order, and Kirkgordon gave a nod.

"For Alana," Calandra mouthed at him, and waited for his response.

"Thank you," he mouthed back, and watched the black-garbed woman nod to Nefol. The woman and the girl stepped confidently together into the portal and vanished.

Kirkgordon turned to Austerley.

"Come on, Hopalong, it's our turn to dance."

A Small Request

Many thanks for taking the time to read "The Darkness at Dillingham" and I hope you enjoyed it as much as I did writing the story. As an Indie author, I am constantly seeking to make more people aware of my writing. As such I would ask that if you enjoyed "The Darkness at Dillingham" please leave a review so others will know about the dynamic that is the Austerley & Kirkgordon world.

Kind regards,
Gary

Bonus Chapter: Chapter 1 of Dagon's Revenge, A&K #3

There was a soft crunch underfoot and Kirkgordon looked down to see charcoal soil beneath. Amongst the occasional rocks, long sprouts of wild grass were growing, or rather, existing, for the grass didn't protrude like massed ranks of spearmen but instead had a lazy limpness to it. There were no trees, just miles of undulating small hills like those he had seen around Belfast. Drumlins, the good folk there called them, but their scenery was green and lush from the abundant rainfall. Here was just bleak.

Calandra's black leather jacket and dark jeans made her almost fade into the scenery. He watched her survey the land, the ponytail of her long black hair waving from side to side. Her beauty was out of place here but he was glad to have her along for the ride. It wasn't just her fighting skills, which were a match for anyone he knew, but also the comfort of a woman whom he fought hard to see as a close sister and not a potential lover. No matter the place, she always looked good.

"Does Mr Austerley know where we are?" asked Havers, letting Kirkgordon know that his whole party had crossed through the portal from the Russian countryside to… to… well, to here, wherever *here* was.

"Give me a minute," grunted Austerley. "Only just bloody

arrived."

"Nefol, Cally – do a little scout and come back in five minutes. See if there's anything around here," ordered Kirkgordon.

"Or any*one*," said Havers.

Nefol, though only a slip of a girl at twelve years of age, nodded with a grimness that a child of her age should not possess. Although she was "functioning well" in Calandra's words, it was evident that her father's death was taking its toll. Kirkgordon had watched Father Jonah be burnt to ashes by Farthington's breath, and he still struggled to shake the image. But she didn't seem to have vengeance on her mind. Unlike Havers.

"Mr Kirkgordon, how do you intend to find our target if we don't know where we are?"

Havers hadn't been impressed when Ma'am gave me control of this mission, thought Kirkgordon. And he's going to snipe whenever he can. "Since when is Farthington our target, Mr Havers?" Kirkgordon sniggered to himself. Major Havers hated to be called a Mister. "This is a rescue mission for Alana. The moment we get her, we leave. It's my call all the way, Mr Havers. Remember that."

"And *you* remember what that bastard dragon did to the priest." Havers stepped away, pretending to survey the local area. Austerley tapped Kirkgordon on the shoulder.

"Getting out of here soon-as is a good idea, Churchy. I think I know where we are but I'm not one hundred percent certain. Look how wasted everything is. This place has seen the Elders at some point. This decay isn't natural."

"Indy, I just walked through a portal from Russia to here. I kinda left natural behind. Anyway, maybe when daytime comes it'll be easier."

"Churchy, this *is* daytime!"

"What?" Kirkgordon looked around. "But it's so dark."

"Can you feel the thickness in the air? Even that is decayed, full of pollution. I think nightfall is going to bring a proper darkness."

"How's the foot?" asked Kirkgordon, looking at the booted appendage.

"Sore. And too small. But there's something else."

Hell, thought Kirkgordon, this won't be good. First he loses his foot, blaming me for pinning it with an arrow before Farthington ripped it off his leg. Then he somehow magics a foot off a witch but it's too small and has gone ebony black as it's full of evil. Now what?

"The foot has been tingling," said Austerley, "ever since we arrived. Just tingling."

"Which means?"

"How should I know, Churchy? It's my first evil foot, dammit."

"So, where are we?" asked Kirkgordon, trying to give Austerley a chance to talk about something he did know.

"Well, it's hard to say in English, there's no translation. Closest is probably the Nether Lands."

"Holland? How is this Holland?"

"Hardly. In the scrolls buried deep in the vaults of the St Basil church of the Nazarene, deep set into the Andes, the name given is—"

Kirkgordon heard the noises but they were not like any language he knew. Deciding not to ask for a linguistics lesson from Austerley, Kirkgordon changed tactics.

"So you know about this place. Good, Indy, we're going to need it. What can you tell me about it?"

"Not much," said Austerley, and Kirkgordon's face fell. "But I wouldn't holiday here."

But Austerley would go anywhere to look at this occult stuff, thought Kirkgordon. We must be in trouble.

Calandra emerged from behind a small hillock and raced up to Kirkgordon.

"Time to move, Churchy. There's a whole horde of... of... well, a whole horde of something coming along a road just over there. And I think they will be passing right by us."

"Get Nefol, Cally. Havers, we're moving out."

Three people glided quickly and quietly across the barren terrain to lie behind a small hump by the road. One other followed, hauling a large man in an awkward fashion. The man being dragged emitted grunts and expletives as they travelled.

So much for the road, thought Kirkgordon. A track was probably a better description, as only a slight wearing of the ground indicated the path. But he could hear footsteps coming. Well, he could hear something coming. There was a noise and it included multiple sounds, but not footsteps. Hiding behind the hump, Kirkgordon signalled his team to have their weapons at the ready before taking an arrow from his quiver. The markings on the feathers told him its function, and he smiled at the idea that presented itself. He recognized the sound coming. He could hear hopping.

Kirkgordon held Austerley's head to the ground so that he couldn't peer too far over the terrain and alert others to their presence. The rest of the group could be trusted and Kirkgordon flashed a *How many?* sign to Havers. *Thirty to forty* came the reply. Better not to get noticed.

Soon Kirkgordon's eyeline was dominated by humanoid figures that looked like upright frogs. They were the fully developed counterparts of those he had seen on the Scottish island, and most had lost all traces of humanity. The eyes were bloated and the legs were spindly below the knee but wide at the thigh. Webbed feet kicked up dust as they hopped. At least there must be water, thought Kirkgordon. These things couldn't survive in this dryness.

Looking at the rest of the team, Kirkgordon was not surprised to sense uneasiness in Calandra and Havers. Both had nearly lost their lives to these creatures before. Nefol was sullen-facedly staring at the parade. Several times Austerley tried to raise his head only to find it gently pushed back down by Kirkgordon, who had witnessed Austerley's negative reactions too many times. Most fire brigades would kill to have a siren like an Austerley breakdown.

The creatures were almost out of view when they suddenly stopped. One of the frog-men left the front of the party and joined a taller frog-man at the rear. There were various croaks and shakes of their heads, then a harsher croak brought the whole party around. They started to hop as one towards the hump that hid Kirkgordon and Austerley.

"Churchy!" came a hushed whisper.

"Not now, Indy!"

"But my foot, it's pounding. It's vibrating. Moving."

Kirkgordon looked down and saw the boot over Austerley's black foot rippling like a wave across its surface. His eyes widened as the foot swelled and contracted. Looking back up, he saw the frog-men hopping frantically towards their position.

"Cally! Havers! Grab Austerley and run. That way. And don't stop until you're clear of me."

His partners did not hesitate, each linking an arm under

Austerley's and dragging the former professor away. Austerley was stunned at first but then he began to shout.

"My foot. It's pounding. It's pulsing. Look my foot!"

Nefol stood beside Kirkgordon with her staff at the ready, but Kirkgordon rounded on her.

"Get away, Nefol, go. Leave me. I know what I'm doing."

Looking up, Nefol saw the frog-man horde drawing closer, less than twenty metres away now. The young girl shook her head and focused on the oncoming targets.

"Nefol! Oh heck, hang on then." Kirkgordon stepped across Nefol, placing himself between the horde and the girl. She watched him draw his bow and saw the markings on the feathers. Dropping to her knees, she placed herself at Kirkgordon's heels and grabbed his legs with one hand, planting her staff into the ground with the other.

The horde was ten metres away when Kirkgordon loosed the arrow. The lead frog-man had just taken to the air with a large push from his massive thighs and the arrow sailed past him. It looked like Kirkgordon had lost this battle. The creature continued its flight and was in its downward arc, arms raised and about to land on Kirkgordon's head when the arrow pierced the ground some twenty metres away.

The frog-man felt a pull from behind, as if a lasso had reached out and grabbed his body. For a moment he was held suspended in the air, then he started to edge backwards. Kirkgordon smiled as he watched the horde being dragged into the vortex that the arrow had produced. A mighty wind blew past his shoulders and he felt Nefol clutching him tightly. He crouched in front of her to block her progress towards the vortex. One by one, the frog-men were whipped from their feet into the newly formed abyss, a howling sound accompanying their demise.

Kirkgordon knew that the vortex had no effect on the shooter, but he was also aware that everyone around him would get pulled towards it. Inside his head, a little doubt banged upon the door and asked whether his friends had gotten far enough away. After all, there was so little vegetation or solid matter to grab onto. Watching the last frog-man disappear into the blackness, he heard shouts from Austerley and Havers. The hole was closing back up but the pair raced past him like they were on invisible carts. When the vortex collapsed, Austerley was five metres in front of Kirkgordon, face down in the dirt. Havers was lying on his back, having spread himself in an attempt to slow his progress.

"I told you to cling to the staff." Turning, Kirkgordon saw Calandra with a scold on her face, her eyes pinned on Austerley. Her black wings were spread open and she gave off a regal air, looking like a Valkyrie. "Nefol, are you okay?"

The young girl nodded and released her grip on Kirkgordon. Havers stood up, glanced around, and brushed the dirt from his outfit.

"Well, I guess that was good thinking, Mr Kirkgordon, but shall we proceed?"

"In a minute, Mr Havers," Kirkgordon replied. "There are a few things to consider first." Kirkgordon turned to Nefol, who smiled back at him.

"Next time, Nefol, if I say run, then you run."

Nefol's face turned sullen. "Next time, then, kindly tell your team what you are doing." Before Kirkgordon could answer, Nefol moped off towards Calandra, who was giving Kirkgordon a mother's look of *Was that really necessary?*

"And as for you, Indy," said Kirkgordon, "what's the deal with your foot? It was like it was drawing the frog-men to it."

Austerley nodded and, although still winded, started to speak.

"Yes... I think so... We are in the Nether lands."

"Holland?" asked Calandra.

"No! The back lands. It doesn't translate well. Creatures, things here... it's like they're drawn to evil, or so I've read. I don't know how, but they know. And that damn witch was full of evil."

"Don't start that, Indy. You took the foot," scolded Kirkgordon.

As Austerley snarled at Kirkgordon, Havers suggested a solution.

"Well, this would appear to be an unnecessary risk. I suggest removal of the appendage."

"How?" asked Kirkgordon.

"What do you mean, how? No one's taking my foot off!"

"Shush, Indy. How, Havers?"

"I have a blade, Mr Kirkgordon, and you know I can handle a blade."

"Churchy, you keep that lunatic off me. Havers, you've been psycho since the priest got burnt. No one's taking my foot off me."

"Indy, not in front of her," raged Calandra as Nefol stormed off.

"Bloody magic, Indy," spat Kirkgordon. "Five minutes in and you guys are at each other."

"Well, shall I?" asked Havers.

"No!" shouted Austerley.

"No. Not yet, Mr Havers. We are in the clear at the moment," answered Kirkgordon.

"But for how long?"

"Long enough. But I'll bear your suggestion in mind."

"No you bloody won't," interjected Austerley.

"Enough!" Kirkgordon looked for Calandra and found her a little distance away. "Give Austerley a hand, will you?" he called to her. "And then we'd better get moving."

"Okay, Indy, but where?"

"Austerley, you know where we are, but do you know it exactly?" asked Kirkgordon.

"No, nothing except that this is the Nether... back lands."

"Well, the frog-men came from down that way, so there must be something there," said Kirkgordon. "Let's find out what it is."

Acknowledgements

To Janet for her enthusiasm for my writing and giving me space to keep on knocking out the weird notions in my head.

To my wonderful children who give their Dad some space and for letting me be in their story.

To Al, for continued friendship and Austerleyness!

To everyone who comments and feeds back on the initial workings I hand out, it makes it that much easier.

To Jake for the most excellent artwork, Caroline for the sheen on the novel.

To Peter Urpeth and Emergents, thanks for the continued support and help.

As always, to the fantastic American gentleman who mis-heard my friend's name and then sent a package to a certain Mr Austerley. Your error was a gaff of genius.

To Kathleen and the Stornoway Writer's Group. Thanks for all the encouragement and honesty.

To God who gave me this creative talent, may He watch over me like He watches over Kirkgordon.

About the Author

GR Jordan is a self-published author who finally decided at forty that in order to have an enjoyable lifestyle, his creative beast within would have to be unleashed. His books mirror that conflict in life where acts of decency contend with self-promotion, goodness stares in horror at evil and kindness blind-sides us when we are at our worst. Corrupting our world with his parade of wondrous and horrific characters, he highlights everyday tensions with fresh eyes whilst taking his methodical, intelligent mainstays on a roller-coaster ride of dilemmas, all the while suffering the banter of their provocative sidekicks.

A graduate of Loughborough University where he masqueraded as a chemical engineer but ultimately played American football, GR Jordan worked at changing the shape of cereal flakes and pulled a pallet truck for a living. Watching vegetables freeze at -40'C was another career highlight and he was also one of the Scottish Highlands' "blind" air traffic controllers. Having flirted with most places in the UK, he is now based in the

Isle of Lewis in Scotland where his free time is spent between raising a young family with his wife, writing, figuring out how to work a loom and caring for a small flock of chickens. Luckily his writing is influenced by his varied work and life experience as the chickens have not been the poetical inspiration he had hoped for!

You can connect with me on:

- http://www.grjordan.com
- https://www.twitter.com/carpetless
- https://www.facebook.com/carpetlessleprechaun

Subscribe to my newsletter:

- http://www.grjordan.com/download-footsteps

Also by G R Jordan

G R Jordan writes fantasy books in several series, including the Austerley & Kirkgordon series of which you have just read the third of its origin stories. At the time of publishing there are 3 origin stories and 3 full length novels with more planned in the near future. Published books are detailed below, including the feel good fantasy series, Island Adventures.

Crescendo!: An Austerley & Kirkgordon Adventure #1
A shape-shifting dragon. A cult bringing forth a nightmare. Two broken men, separated by hatred, must bind together to save the world.

Bitter-sweet partners, Austerley and Kirkgordon, take on the darkness to prevent a displaced people ending the world. If you like bizarre creatures, fast paced action and cataclysmic nightmares, you'll love G R Jordan's first novel. Get the book readers have called "a fast paced gothic thriller with lots of humour" and "refreshingly modern take on Lovecraftian themes."

Can the Elder darkness be stopped? It's the blasphemous fanfare for the end of the world!

Dagon's Revenge: An Austerley & Kirkgordon Adventure #3

A shattered hero races to save his wife. A rescue team falling apart. Elder god Dagon's coming back and he's pissed!

Kirkgordon takes his team beyond our world in this third instalment in the Austerley & Kirkgordon urban fantasy series. If you like danger and desire, punchy dialogue and cataclysmic nightmares then you'll love G R Jordan's bunch of discombobulated heroes.

Sometimes, there are no good choices!

Cally: Austerley & Kirkgordon Origins #2

A village emptied of its children. A warrior finding her greatest desire. But a witch's vengeance wrecks a curse that will devastate her forever.

The tale of Calandra's curse is the 2nd story in the A&K origins series, a collection of short stories that expand G R Jordan's A&K universe. If you love rollicking action, imperfect heroes and extraordinary, magical villains, then you will love the Austerley & Kirkgordon series.

Yesterday, he offered her the rest of his life. Today a vengeful witch wants to take him away. Can Calandra's dreams survive the mother of all storms?

Sometimes a woman can be too cold for any man!

The People in the Pool: Austerley & Kirkgordon Origins #3

He lost her, murdered a long time ago. But now she's returned. If something isn't real, does it matter?

"The People in the Pool" is the 3rd origin story in the A&K origins series that expand G R Jordan's A&K universe. If you love rollicking action, imperfect heroes and weird villains and places, then you will love the Austerley & Kirkgordon series.

Not every mother can warm a child's heart.

Surface Tensions: Island Adventures #1

Mermaids sighted near a Scottish island. A town exploding in anger and distrust. And Donald's got to get the sexiest fish in town, back in the water.

"Surface Tensions" is the first story in a series of Island adventures from the pen of G R Jordan. If you love comic moments, cosy adventures and light fantasy action, then you'll love these tales with a twist.

Get the book that amazon readers said, "perfectly captures life in the Scottish Hebrides" and that explores "human nature at its best and worst".

Something's stirring the water!